THE *IMPOSSIBLE* CHOICE

RITA H ROWE

For Mum, who planted the seed of an idea for this story which took hold and I completely bastardised. Sorry and thank you.

And of course, for John.

I guess you never really know if you're loved.

Only the person who loves knows.

The other believes or chooses to believe or chooses not to believe.

CONTENTS

PROLOGUE

1963

His arm hung limply across the wall of the bathtub; his head rolled forward towards his chest in an acute angle. His eyes were closed and she remembered thinking that it was a relief she didn't have to face him, that he couldn't see her reaction. What would he have expected to see? Shock? Hurt? Fear?

When she walked into the bathroom and saw his lifeless body immersed in water that was stained the colour of her blouse, she barely flinched. She realised later that it was shock, a disbelief that caused her to stop in her tracks and tilt her head slightly to assess the situation. She moved slowly to the bathtub, his body neatly encased in it, and knelt on the floor, somewhat aware that her bare knees were damp. She reached for his hand and knew that she mustn't touch it. Other people would have to deal with it, morgue people. But she couldn't resist running her fingers along the side of his face, moving his hair away from his eyes. She never liked when his hair fell over them. It made him look messy, a bad boy, which he was anything but. But he had been bad, for the first time since she had known him; for all of their nine years, he had never been bad, until now.

She raised herself off the cream tiles and walked slowly

away from the scene, not looking behind her. She closed the bathroom door behind her, relieved that the last of the boarders had left the previous night. She was glad Lucille was at school, and Marina, not yet seven, was still asleep. She tried not to think of them, growing up now without a father. She would have time enough to deal with it all later. There were more important things to do. Two bookings would need to be cancelled and she would have to make some calls. She couldn't think about grieving right now. There would be plenty of time for that later too. She headed into the kitchen to make the call to the police. It was going to be a long day.

CHAPTER 1

1972

This is absurd, Mary thought, as she closed the door and leaned against it, her head spinning. He was nine years her junior; she had no business messing around with him. But loneliness does something to a person, and she slid to the floor, her head on her bended knees, savouring his touch, the gentle palm on her cheek, the way he reached his head so close to hers, close enough for her to smell the peppermint tea, a treat and one she could ill afford to give away for free.

She had leapt off the armchair and bolted straight to her room, now wishing she had the guts to stay, to see it through, to let him kiss her. It had been leading up to this for a long time, nearly a year, and she clenched her hands in frustration. Gary wouldn't have minded at all; he'd been gone for more than nine years and he would have wanted her to be happy, to be loved again. Mary had vowed never to love another man, to be faithful to the memory of her dead husband. But now here was Lawrence, *young* Lawrence, and the temptation was strong.

'Mum?' Her head jerked up at the sound and saw the shadowed head of Lucille raised from the bed.

'Go back to sleep, love,' she whispered, afraid Marina

3

would wake too. But Marina could usually sleep through anything. It was Lucille who waited until she had packed up for the night before she could settle down for the night.

'Can I sleep with you tonight?' Even at seventeen, Lucille liked to snuggle next to her mother, especially when they all shared a room. Usually Mary welcomed her with open arms, especially when Marina got to snoring too loudly. It was nice to feel needed, by at least one of her daughters.

'No, my angel,' said Mary, raising herself off the floor with some effort. The skin on her face was still tingling from his touch and she tried to shake the image of him from her brain. It wouldn't do for her girls to see her in this state. It would unnerve them. 'Marina would be lonely without you.'

'But Marina doesn't wake up at all,' Lucille protested. 'Look.' She bobbed about on the bed and the black curls of Marina bounced around, but she didn't stir.

Mary stifled a laugh and was tempted, but tonight she wanted to savour the moment from earlier, to think about each thing that happened, step by step. 'Not tonight, Lu,' she replied and reached forward, softly caressing her daughter's cheek.

'Okay, Mum,' said Lucille, and through the light that shone from the moon into the little room, she saw her daughter smile in resignation.

How she loved these beautiful creatures, the only gifts left to her from her dead husband. Them, and this place, which was more a burden than a blessing. She had to work so hard just to keep it, but she did, had managed by herself to keep the boarding house running, the dream she and Gary had worked so hard towards.

She tiptoed to the window to close the curtain but

instead leaned her warm forehead on the cool pane, looking into the night—her little cloistered world, which she hadn't left since his death. This idyllic beach haven, which was yet to be discovered by the rich entrepreneurs who would eventually find it and dot it with hotels and caravan parks. She couldn't leave here, ever. It was hers ... and his. Her heart was heavy. Was she ever going to say goodbye to him? She had to; she had to live again, to move on. But with Lawrence? She would be the laughingstock of Righteous Creek. She could just hear the whispers, the rumours, the idle gossip as she walked to the corner store. Righteous indeed; self-righteous was more like it.

Her and Lawrence! That would give them all something to gossip about. She sighed. They gossiped anyway, since as long as she could remember. From the moment she could understand words, she understood that she was not the same as everyone, that her parents had left a bad taste in the mouths of the good people of the Creek. And when Gary had swept her off her feet, Gary, in his crisp uniform, Gary, who donned his dashing smile for anyone and everyone, Gary, who treated everyone, from the help to his boss, in the same way, they forgave her for being the offspring of drunks, of people who had no time for anyone, not even their own child.

She stepped out into the silent hall and ran her fingers along the lid of the piano. She hadn't played in ... well, since his death. She was tempted to open it now, to put her fingers on the ivory keys, but she knew she couldn't. She had tried before but it made her heart ache for him so terribly, she couldn't bear it, and wished she were with him, wherever he was.

CHAPTER 2

Gary. She still remembered so clearly the first time she
had laid eyes on him at the concert as she awaited her turn
between the folds of the curtain. She was barely twenty and no
one had caught her attention the way he had, sitting there at the
end of the second row, a man she had never seen before, his eyes
smiling directly at her, as concealed as she was in the shadows of
the stage wing. She had been scanning the rows to find her
parents, to see if they would be in the audience for once, and she
always felt a stab of disappointment when she realised they were
never going to attend any of the piano recitals she gave. Her eyes
returned to Gary as she backed into the side of the stage and
found his eyes settled on her with such fascination, her heart
bumped loudly and she scrambled backwards into the line of
nervous performers behind her.

'Sorry,' she muttered, amidst a murmuring of moans and
curses.

'What's up?' Virginia moved her violin into the crook of
Mary's back to keep her from turning them all into dominoes.

'Nothing. Sorry,' she said again and Virginia moved her
head around Mary's shoulder to find the cause of her reaction.
Mary pushed her shoulder backwards and with it, Virginia's
chin.

'Whatever,' said Virginia and Mary tried to ignore her. Virginia had been the bane of Mary's high school years and still she wouldn't leave her alone, even after high school was done more than two years before.

Mary's hands were clammy now and she opened and squeezed them shut, trying to loosen her nerves, wishing she didn't have to go on next, but the programme had to be followed. She never had anyone come to see her perform except for Mrs Davis, her piano teacher, who was more like a mother than her own, and she always sat in the front row, her eyes glittering with pride when Mary took to the stage.

'Our next act on the piano, reciting Beethoven's Moonlight Sonata, is Mary Shillder.'

Mary stepped forward, tentatively, trying not to look towards the man whose eyes had so keenly stared at her, and headed to the upright, which was placed in the corner of the stage. She sat down and adjusted her skirt, using it to discreetly wipe the sweat off her palms, and took a deep breath.

The second her fingers touched the keys, all of what existed beyond the instrument disappeared. She was lost in the music, her body swaying to the rise and fall of the tempo, her eyes nearly closed in a state of passion and once it hit its crescendo, she almost fell into despair knowing it was nearly at an end. When she hit the last note, she let out a breath. Unwilling to take her fingers away from the instrument, she finally let herself become aware of where she was. There was but a moment's silence, and suddenly, a gust of applause, something she still was not accustomed to. She hesitated, embarrassed, but could hear Mrs Davis's voice call her name. She stood up and turned to the audience, smiling down at her teacher, who, as usual, had great big tears rolling down her cheeks. Mrs Davis smiled, a toothy, shameless smile, back at her. Mary eyes moved to the left, in automation, and landed on the man who had his hands forward, clapping loudly, bellowing 'Brava'.

Her nerves got the better of her again and she stumbled as she put her foot behind her. An audible gasp from the crowd was the last thing she heard before she hit the panelled floor. Scrambling to her feet quickly, she made her way to the safety of the curtains without looking back into the crowd, and leaned on the wall, taking a deep breath.

She let her nerves thaw as she watched Virginia in her full red skirt and black kitten heels swish to the centre of the stage, placing her violin against her shoulder with a flourish. She envied her poise, her clothes, her glossy blonde hair that was set with such precision, a well-placed curl falling onto her forehead, her perfectly coiffed bob in line with her shoulders. Mary tried not to let those things matter, but she couldn't help but be a little jealous that the man in the audience would have forgotten her existence when Princess Virginia stepped on the stage. She sighed.

'Are you okay?'

Mary jumped and turned to see the man standing behind her. 'Uh-huh.' She swallowed a surge of saliva that invaded her mouth. 'Just nerves,' she muttered.

'You were wonderful,' he said and Mary raised her eyes to his. Grey twinkling ones stared back into hers. He was so close she could smell a light scent of cologne, nothing she could place, but she had the sudden urge to get closer to it, to him.

'That's Virginia,' she said, not knowing why she did, nodding to the stage.

'Uh-huh,' he said without taking his eyes off her, and Mary thought she would stumble again. She grabbed at the wall behind her to steady herself. One fall was enough for one night.

'I'm okay,' she said and tried to smile.

'You're more than okay,' he replied with a curl of his lips. 'I'm going to marry you.'

Mary wasn't sure she heard right but the smile that remained on his face grew wider and she felt her cheeks heat. 'I have to go,' she mumbled and pushed past him. She clambered through the black curtains and down the stage to the dressing room. There was no reason for her to go to the dressing room; it wasn't like she had to change her clothes, but she had to get there, away from what had just transpired. She moved past the bundle of women coming in and out and stood against a wall at the far end, begging for her heart to return to its normal rhythm.

Who was that man and why did he have such an effect on her, or her on him, for that matter? It wasn't as if she didn't have boys and men trying their luck with her, from the café where she worked to the library where she spent time trying to educate herself in the business of fashion, a dream she knew would never materialise. She just didn't have an interest in them and once wondered if she just wasn't attracted to men. But she was not interested in the same sex either, and as she watched classmates and co-workers fall in love, sometimes on many occasions, she thought that perhaps there was something wrong with her.

She tried to feel something, tried to get lost in the moment when Matt, the young man whom she'd met at a dance some two years ago, put his lips on hers. But all she felt were the cracked lips that grazed her own, and long arms that clutched her too tight. It lasted two months, Mary trying in vain to feel what everyone else was talking about. She allowed him to caress her breasts, cringing as he did, and when her affections for him were not deepened by any measure, she gave up and asked a sulking and insulted Matt to leave her alone. He did eventually, after trying in vain to woo her back with flowers and chocolates, which she promptly gave to Mrs Davis. Once he realised that she had made up her mind, he called her a frigid princess and ignored her whenever they passed each other on the street, and he never again set foot inside the café in which she worked. And Mary focused on working, saving money for her piano lessons, putting a little away for when she would have to move out of home.

Now here she was, her heart pounding, her breath short, and there was no one whom she could talk to about how she was feeling. But it struck her that she was actually feeling something she had never felt before, something she had yearned for, thought about and worried about. She didn't even know his name. Well, why would she? They had barely exchanged a few words. And did she hear right? Did he say he was going to marry her? She frowned. The nerve of him! Then her eyebrows creased in bewilderment. Maybe she hadn't heard right after all. Who on earth would tell someone that the first time they met them?

'Who was that guy?' Virginia popped out of nowhere and cornered Mary.

'I don't know,' said Mary quite honestly. She wished she could talk to Virginia, but she had been burned by her too many times.

'He's hot!' Virginia raised her eyes to the ceiling and fanned her face with her hand, and Mary felt herself wanting to scratch out those pretty blue eyes, a feeling she'd never experienced before, certainly not out of jealousy. 'I'm going back out to introduce myself. I've never seen him around before.' She walked to the mirrors, patting her perfect hair, and sashayed to the door. 'He's out here now,' she said, turning back to Mary with a giggle.

Mary nodded glumly and, placing herself on a stool, stared at herself in the mirror. She was good-looking, she knew that from the attention she received, but she didn't stand a chance next to the over-dressed, over-made-up Virginia. She pushed back her black wavy hair and stared into her big brown eyes, wishing they could sparkle blue like Virginia's. She wished she had put on a little makeup, done her hair up in a bun as Mrs Davis suggested, but Mary didn't expect to meet this man tonight. 'It's always the last place you expect to meet the man of your dreams that you do,' Mrs Davis had said one day when reminiscing about meeting her husband at a funeral. Yes, Mrs Davis was right, but how could she be sure this was the man of her dreams? He certainly was wonderful to look at, the sound of his voice, the scent of his ... There was no point thinking about that now.

She sighed and stood up, smoothing out her blue skirt and straightening her black belt, which she borrowed from Mrs Davis, who had put another hole in it so it would wrap neatly around Mary's waist. She wanted to go straight home and try to savour the feeling of her fingers on the piano and forget the image of the face that was beginning to imprint itself in her brain. But she knew she must do the right thing and go back into the audience to watch the rest of the show and support the rest of the acts, of which there were only a few left.

Besides, what was there really for her at home, if that was what she could call it? Her parents were already talking about moving to Perth and Mary wondered if it was just their way of moving away from her. She would deal with that obstacle when it arose. Mrs Davis had already offered her a home in the abode of her and her husband, but she couldn't put her out, knowing it was cramped enough already and they couldn't afford to have another person live with them, even if she did pay her way.

She opened the door, the hopeful part of herself half expecting the man to still be standing there, but her heart dropped when he was nowhere in sight, knowing Virginia must have won him over. She walked around to the back of the hall and watched as another performer sat at the piano, her hands moving across the keys.

'Why is she playing the same song you did?' She heard his voice so close to her ear. A shiver ran down Mary's spine and her arms filled with goosebumps but she didn't respond. 'Sounds terrible now,' he continued.

Mary wanted to laugh but she could feel the heat from his closeness and shivered instead. 'She's good,' she replied, wanting to keep him talking to her.

'I could listen to *you* all day,' said his voice and Mary felt a flush of pleasure run through her body. A shush could be heard from a woman in the last row and he chuckled. Mary wondered where Virginia had gotten to and how she hadn't been able to snare him away. 'I could listen to you all day,' he said again. 'And all night, if you marry me.'

Another shush and the turn of a couple of heads. Mary turned abruptly to him and felt her forehead knock the bottom of his chin. 'Be quiet,' she whispered.

'I will. When you kiss me.'

The shushing woman turned her whole body around and glared at them. Mary realised he was not going to stop talking, so she pushed past him and walked out into the foyer. He was right behind her when she turned around and before she knew it, his lips were on hers. Electricity flooded through her body and she could feel her knees begin to crumble. She took hold of herself, stood up straight and slapped his cheek.

He stepped back with the force of the blow and put his hand to the assaulted cheek which was quickly reddening. 'I guess I deserved that,' he said sheepishly.

'Yes, you did,' said Mary, not sure if she was angry or excited; she just knew if she didn't do something, she would collapse. She strode to the door and walked into the cool air, hoping against hope she hadn't put him off, that he would follow her. She stood out there for a few moments and heard the door open behind her.

'Hello, Mary,' he said. 'My name is Gary. It's nice to meet you.'

CHAPTER 3

1972

Mary walked back into her room and paused at the stairs. Her mind went back to Lawrence, her heart giving a thump at the thought of him, a little reminder that she was being unfaithful to the man who still had her heart. She undressed and slid into bed, loneliness filling it like never before. She wondered what Lawrence was doing; was he thinking about what happened before too? Or was she just being vain; had she been deprived of a man's touch for too long? She knew if she wanted to, she could find one easily; she got catcalls and propositions many times, but she had never felt the slightest inclination to take any of them up on it and started dressing in the dowdiest manner to avert attention from herself. Flings had never been her thing, not even when she was a teenager, and she certainly didn't have the time or energy for them now.

Now all she had were the girls, Gary's legacy, and this place, Jesse's Boarding House, named after their son, lost before he was born. She knew that was the nail in the coffin for Gary. It was when his moods had begun to swing more often and even her touch on his hand or face could not raise him out of his reverie as she sometimes had the ability to. She had to ignore her own suffering, the nine months of anticipation, the pain of birthing a child that was torn from her, blue and still, and the heartache that followed had to be kept to herself—a moment of release in the shower, where she could let the tears roll down her face as she clutched to the shower curtain, a walk along the beach in the middle of the quiet night where no one could hear her cries but the waves. Because she had to keep it together; Gary had gone to pieces and she had to be both parents to her girls who couldn't understand why their father didn't throw them up in the air anymore or chase them around the beach, or sit on the sofa, one of them on each side of him, safe in their father's arms.

She turned again in her bed and clutched at her pillow, willing herself to go to sleep. She could hear snores through the walls and couldn't help but chuckle inwardly. The Davises were a funny couple. They had moved into the boarding house almost immediately after it had been opened and Mary was happy to be able to repay the kindness shown to her by her former piano teacher. Mr Davis, nearly seventy, was the first one who arrived at the dining hall every morning, his eyes red, complaining about his loud wife. And Mrs Davis, a little younger than her husband, would appear around an hour later, looking like a queen, a bright smile on a fully made-up face, ready to take the dog for his beach stroll. Dogs were not usually allowed in the boarding house, but the Davises were permanent boarders and Poopy, the little Jack Russell, was very unlike others of his breed. A sweet, calm temperament, he cosied up to guests, and barely barked. Of course, he wasn't supposed to sleep in the rooms, but most guests, and Mary herself, turned a blind eye when Mrs Davis left her door open after dinner and Poopy sneaked in, magically appearing in the backyard by morning.

There was Sophie, not much younger than Mary, who travelled often, but always found her way back here to Jesse's Boarding. Mary liked Sophie, who would often sit with her by the fire and tell her tales of her exploits. A small-time actress,

Sophie was going to make it big someday, living in hope that time would not run out before she caught a break. But for now, she was taking bit parts in small movies and sometimes landing a theatre gig. She wasn't wealthy and readily admitted that she was happy to take jewellery and gifts offered by rich men who were enamoured with her beauty and liked her hanging off their arms. She didn't give them anything more than a peck on the cheek for their trouble, and if they wanted more, she had a good strong knee that could aim very well. Sophie had some wonderful stories and Mary looked forward to her arriving at the boarding house, not ever knowing when that may be.

The other four rooms were those that were rented out on a short-term basis, a soft pillow for a weary traveller, visitors to relatives of the Creek, the few people who had discovered it at one stage or another and had come back for the ambience, the beach or just to get away from the business of life. At times, even women who had finally taken too much from their abusive husbands would limp in and Mary would let them stay for a night or two before they returned to their troubled lives. Mary refused their feeble attempts at promises of payment, money she knew they didn't have.

Then there was Lawrence. He lived in Adelaide, only a few hours from Righteous Creek, and he first arrived at Jesse's Boarding for a stopover on the way to Melbourne.

'Melbourne is just a few hours away,' Mary had exclaimed when he'd first come through the door, jangling the little bell atop it. She'd been tidying up after dinner, and the girls were in the lounge with the Davises watching television. 'Why stop now?'

'I'm exhausted,' he replied, loosening his tie. His eyes were bloodshot, but the blue that resembled the sea on a bright day pierced through them. Mary looked away, a little embarrassed at noticing them. 'I know it's late, but do you have a room? I saw the vacancy sign.'

'Yes, of course,' she said and looked at the time. Past nine. It was an uneventful end to spring, the only boarders at the time the Davises. 'My husband is out the back, so I'll just check you in.' It was her usual line for people she didn't know, especially men. On more than one occasion, she'd had to call out for her imaginary husband when a visitor came in drunk or was in a frisky mood.

'Have you had something to eat?' she asked when she saw him eye the complimentary cookies on the desk.

'Not really,' he said and licked his lips. 'I've just driven from Port Lincoln, almost ten hours straight. Barely stopped to … you know.'

Mary blushed.

'Sorry to be crass,' he said.

'Don't worry about it.' She gave him the key to Room 6, the one on the side of the house with a direct view of the ocean. 'There is some leftover pot roast. Are you okay with that?'

'That sounds amazing,' he replied, his eyes lighting up.

'Put away your things, and I'll get it ready.' She gestured to the stairs. 'Third room to the right.' She pointed to the left. 'Dining's in there.'

'Thank you,' he said and took out his wallet.

'You can pay when you leave,' she said, hoping he would stay more than one day and knowing he probably had somewhere to be tomorrow. *Stop it!* she reprimanded herself, surprised at her thoughts, her sudden attraction to this stranger making her uneasy.

She was just setting down his plate when he walked in wearing a different shirt, his hair combed back. Even his eyes seemed less tired, and when they caught sight of the hot food on the table, they lit up.

He looked around at the empty dining hall. 'Sorry I'm putting you out.'

'Not at all. Dinner is served at six, but it's no problem,' said Mary. 'Water?'

He nodded. 'Thank you.' He sat at the table, crossed himself in a little prayer and began to eat. Mary wasn't sure if she should stay; she didn't want him to eat by himself, but he may also want to be by himself. She turned to leave after placing a glass of water beside his plate.

'Keep me company … please?'

Mary felt her heart skip a beat and turned back. She sat two chairs away from him and he looked at his plate, trying not to smile. Mary blushed, again astonished that she wanted to talk to this man whom she had just met and was more surprised she was finding it hard to make conversation.

'So, er, what do you do, Lawrence?'

'I work for a trucking company. My father's,' he said ruefully. 'I don't drive trucks, but I do have to travel often, usually between Melbourne and Adelaide, sometimes Sydney, but not there too much. Once I even travelled to Perth. That was a hike!'

Mary's back straightened at the mention of Perth and

she noticed Lawrence pause and look at her quizzically. 'That's a lot of driving,' she replied, trying to cover her reaction. This man was more perceptive than most.

'What about you …?'

'Mum!' Lucille bounced into the room and almost skidded at the sight of Lawrence. She turned to her mother, then back to the man whose eyes were raised in amusement at this teenage hurricane.

'Lucille!' She creased her brows. The girls usually stayed away from new guests, mainly for their own protection. Mary had warned them, but in all fairness, Lucille wouldn't have known a stranger checked in and had dinner this late. 'This is Lawrence. He's here for the night.'

Lucille blushed and began to sway awkwardly against the dining chair. 'Hello, Lawrence,' she said, a queer lilt in her voice, and Mary wanted to roll her eyes at her daughter's flirty behaviour.

'Hello, Lucille,' he replied, smiling at her as if he didn't notice she was acting like a lovesick girl, gawking at him. 'Nice to meet you.'

'Nice to meet you too.' Lucille froze for a moment, and turned and almost ran out of the room.

'Yes … well,' said Mary and saw his face change into something she couldn't quite figure. An expression of discomfort? No, it was more than that. Loss? Grief? But he looked back into his plate and Mary changed the subject. 'Is dinner okay?'

'Delicious,' he said, and she knew he meant it by the way his plate was rapidly clearing.

'Well, I'd better get things ready for the morning. We're having sausages and eggs. Or would you like something else?'

'Nothing for me, thank you. Maybe coffee? I'm not a breakfast person.'

'A bad habit. You do know that it's …'

'The most important meal of the day.' He finished her sentence and chuckled. 'Do you do all meals?'

'Yes, we do. Well, not lunch. Breakfast and dinner, but I think I'm going to turn this into a bed and breakfast only. Most short-term guests don't have dinner here anyway. The streets down the road are beginning to fill with some nice restaurants, new and exotic cuisines that outrival my homely cooking.'

'I would stay for this over a restaurant any day.' He paused and looked at her. 'Besides, the company is much more preferable than eating by oneself.'

Mary blushed and turned from him, running the dishcloth over the already clean counter. She went into the kitchen and leaned over the sink, looking into the darkness of the night. What was she thinking? What was she feeling, especially about a man she'd just met?

'Good night, ma'am,' he called out. 'Thank you for a lovely meal.'

'Good night, Lawrence,' she called back.

****

He was gone the next morning, leaving a note—*I don't even know your name, but thank you* – *LP*—and twice the amount owed. She hoped that meant he was returning that night. He didn't and Mary was disappointed, and more annoyed that she looked out the kitchen window all day, hoping for the sight of him ascending the stairs that led to the reception.

But Lawrence did return a week later, and this time, a suitcase in hand and a wry smile on his face. 'I have a conference in Somerton,' he said. 'It's up the road.'

'I know Somerton,' Mary replied. It was more than just up the road; in fact, more than an hour away, and with its own set of hotels. 'No vacancies there?'

He cleared his throat, lowering his eyes. 'I just preferred to come here.'

Mary busied herself with the papers, trying not to meet his eyes. She was disappointed when he had left the last time, disappearing before she awoke, which was indeed very early. 'You paid too much last week. I can cover the cost of one night. How long will you be staying?'

'Two nights, and no thanks. It was generous of you to let me stay, and feed me, at such late notice.'

'Not at all,' Mary said.

'I loved the room. It was so peaceful. I stayed out on the balcony for hours. That's why I returned here. It's calming.' Mary tried not to smile at the way he was trying to explain himself.

'Well, I'm glad we could accommodate you. The same room is available if you like?'

'That would be great. I have a meeting this afternoon, but I have the evening off. I want to spend it here.'

'Okay,' said Mary, pleased that he enjoyed his last stay, as minimal as it was. 'Dinner is between five thirty and six.'

'When do you eat?'

Mary was taken aback. 'Uh, well, usually when everyone is done. The girls and I sit down together.'

'And your husband? Will he join you today?'

'No, Gary won't be,' she replied, wondering why she didn't just tell him there was no Gary anymore. Perhaps it was too early; maybe she couldn't trust him yet.

'Then maybe if he doesn't mind, I could join you?'

That was unexpected, and the expression on Mary's face, which was more surprise than disapproval, told him he had overstepped. 'No, I mean that I don't eat until later anyway,' Lawrence said as he took the key from her. 'Never mind.' Mary put out her hand to protest, but he picked up his suitcase and walked quickly to his room.

CHAPTER 4

'I like Lawrence,' whispered Lucille as she put the plates in the cupboard, and her mother smiled. Mary had noticed her flirting with the man who sat with them after the other diners, which consisted of the Davises and a couple who were staying for the week, had finished their meal and had settled down for the evening. The Davises usually sat in the lounge until late watching the news or movies and the girls joined them sometimes, but today they remained at the table, Mr Davis eyeing off the hot bread that Lucille brought to the table and Mrs Davis clearly intrigued by this newcomer.

Lawrence had been good, if a little quiet, company. But he was pleasant enough, enquiring about the girls' school, keeping Marina chatting away happily. Mary was pleased to see Marina smile these days. Since she'd turned thirteen, two years before, she had gone into her shell, and the vivacious child she had once been had become a brooding, ill-tempered teenager.

'And what is your favourite subject?' he asked her.

'I'm not fond of any. Maybe music.' She fiddled with her fork, moving it around the plate. 'Mrs Jones is the only nice teacher.'

'What do you want to do with your life? Or are you too young to have that figured out yet?' Mary was impressed with

23

how he was able to keep her talking.

'I'm not too young,' she replied in indignance.

'Oh no, that's not what I mean,' he said. 'Sometimes people don't work out what they want to do for a long time. Many try different things first.'

'Well, I just don't want to be a housewife and rely on men.' She slumped her shoulders and put a piece of steak in her mouth, signalling the end of that conversation.

Lawrence cleared his throat in discomfort and Mary wanted to intervene but she knew Marina would be even more irritated. 'More potatoes?' she interjected.

'I'll have some,' said Mr Davis and Mary reached over to serve him, while his wife looked at him in disapproval. 'Leave me alone, Sylv,' he said without emotion and Mary tried not to smile at the ease in which they conversed. How she wished for that with someone, with Gary. She wanted to grow old with him.

'How about you, Lucille? What year are you in?' Lawrence turned his attention to the awestruck teenager, who for most of the meal had her chin in one hand trying not to stare at him too obviously.

'I'm nearly in year eleven,' said Lucille, sitting up straight and swishing her long locks of dark hair over her shoulder. She had barely touched her food and had gawked at Lawrence since dinner began. Mary tried not to chuckle at her daughter's behaviour, but Lawrence didn't seem to notice, so she didn't reprimand her. It would just embarrass her.

'What is school like these days?' He directed the question at Mary, but Lucille jumped in.

'It's quite the same as when you went, I imagine.'

Mary almost choked on the salad that she had just placed in her mouth. She'd never seen her daughter speak with such poise, so much like an adult, which of course she nearly was. Lawrence looked at Mary in concern and Lucille narrowed her eyes at her mother. Mary coughed into her napkin. 'Sorry, it must have gone down the wrong way,' she said and took a long sip of water. 'Continue, Lucille.'

As Lucille talked about her friends, Mary observed Lawrence. Now she noticed more than his eyes. He sat very straight, his table manners impeccable, his outfit smart but casual, a denim shirt loosely sitting over brown slacks. He wasn't handsome in the traditional sense, his nose slightly large, his hair too long, the way they were wearing it these days, but not something that was attractive to Mary. She preferred slick hair, a neat face, a slender frame—she just wanted Gary. But Lawrence's smile was infectious, and at the table, relaxed, she felt drawn to him. It was nothing she was used to. She had been lonely, she knew that, but she had been lonely for Gary, missed him still, cried into her pillow at night—for him. There was never going to be anyone else, and now she was alarmed. She quickly looked away, flushed and guilty at just the thought of looking at someone else in *that* way.

After dinner, Lawrence helped clear away the dishes, even at the insistence of Mary that he didn't, and Lucille leaned against the doorway and watched, enamoured when he walked up the stairs to his room. Mary giggled to herself again. Lucille had fallen hard. She worried about Lucille sometimes, especially with the flotsam and jetsam that sometimes treaded these hallways. But she trusted her daughter, who was independent and intelligent enough to make good choices. Marina, on the other hand ... only time would tell.

25

Mary tidied the place and went to the lounge where Mr Davis was helping Marina with her maths homework and Lucille lounged, reading a book.

'Everyone okay?' she called and got a variety of responses.

'All good here,' said Sylvia, who was bent over the television changing channels on the dial.

A wave from Lucille.

A nod from Mr Davis, and no answer from Marina.

'I'm going for a walk,' she called and headed out. A walk on the beach was what she needed. It could always clear her mind. She stepped into the moonlight, raising her eyes to the stars, and closed her eyes as the scent of the salty sea air hit her nostrils. She took a deep breath and hopped down the set of steps that led to the sand, pulling her shawl around her. She took off her sandals and felt the cool sand under her feet. She scrunched her toes in them, a feeling of familiarity, of comfort running through her legs and up her body.

She always felt good and hopeful when she strolled on the beach. This wasn't such a bad gig, she thought. She and Gary had saved hard to put a down payment on the place and she was just a couple of years from paying it off. Sure, it didn't bring in very much income, but it was enough for her and the girls. She supplemented her income by sewing clothes and on Sundays, she took them to the market, where a bunch of stalls were laid out on the boardwalk. Sometimes she sold a number of items and sometimes, on quiet weekends, especially when it rained or there was not much happening in Righteous Creek, she didn't sell a thing. But she didn't need much, and the girls understood that they were not going to get every single thing they wanted.

They had been wonderful, caring, loving. She didn't know if she could have survived Gary's death if they had not been there. She knew they missed him too, but Marina seemed to barely remember him, being just seven when he passed. Lucille struggled and she still wanted to talk about him sometimes, and as much as it pained her to do so, Mary was grateful that someone else remembered and loved Gary as she did. His parents, who were against the match, she never heard from, just birthday and Christmas cards for the girls that arrived punctually and which they opened with excitement.

The moon hid behind the clouds but the streetlamps highlighted the few people straggling on the beach. A pair of lovers, holding hands and walking along the shoreline, a lone fisherman, who was not likely to catch anything, a group of teenagers sitting around a bonfire. The chill was beginning to sting now, winter not yet letting go, even though spring had already begun. She wished she had brought a thicker coat with her, but it was probably time to head back anyway. The girls would be finished with their homework and would probably have gone straight to the games room the moment she had left. She smiled, understanding what it was like to be young and allowing a certain amount of flexibility in their lives. Her own youth was filled with so much drama, tension and neglect, she sometimes thought she overcompensated as a mother. But she tried not to think about her parents too often. Those thoughts brought her nothing but pain, and to relive the past was to subject herself to torment. They preferred not to have anything to do with her and she did not have the energy to fight for their love anymore. They only loved each other; she was just a by-product of that love, an unwanted remnant.

She reached the porch and a movement from above

caught her eye. She looked up and saw Lawrence leaning on the railing of his balcony, looking down at her. She shivered, wondering how long he had been there and how long he had been observing her. Up on the balconies there was a perfect view of the stretch of the beach. She sometimes went up there when there were no guests rooming there, just to admire the expanse of the ocean. He was probably doing the very same thing, she thought, embarrassed that she assumed he might have been watching her.

'A lovely evening,' he called to her.

'A little chilly now, but you should take a walk along the beach sometime. It's quite beautiful at sunset.'

'Perhaps you can accompany me? Show me the sights?' He paused. 'Perhaps with your husband?' he added quickly and Mary knew this man was not stupid. He didn't have to be told that her so-called husband didn't exist.

'How about tomorrow?' The words left her mouth before she could stop them and she wished he would decline.

He didn't. 'That would be great.' His voice was low, with a hint of hesitation.

'Yes, that would be nice.' She waved at him. 'Goodnight then.' She quickly scurried back into the house, irritated that her heartbeat had elevated a little.

The next day, Mary went about her work, a lump in her throat, a bunch of butterflies fluttering in her stomach. She was very much looking forward to walking on the beach with Lawrence, but also looking for excuses to avoid it. She didn't want this, to stroll along a moonlit beach with a man who was not Gary. But a part of her wanted to, desperately, and she couldn't understand why. No one had made her feel this way, not for nearly ten years.

The decision was taken out of Mary's hands, as just past midday, a thunderous storm rolled through the bay and by the time Lawrence returned from his conference, the porch was soaked, the beach was wet and the mood was lost. Mary wasn't sure if she was disappointed or relieved; nevertheless, he still came out of his room, smartly dressed, and had dinner with them.

'I will be leaving tomorrow,' said Lawrence, standing in the doorway as Mary dried the dishes alone. The girls had begged to play a couple of board games the Davises were setting out and Mary acquiesced this once. They had flown out of the kitchen, quite happy to be free of the arduous task they performed every evening. 'I wish I had gotten to meet your husband this time.' He moved over to the sink and picked up a dishcloth and a plate from the rack.

Mary bowed her head and her face flushed red. She wished she didn't have to lie, but it was not just for her protection, it was self-preservation. Men tried to flirt with her even with the mention of a husband and it was so much easier to let people know there was a man lurking who would materialise if one of them got out of hand. 'Gary is ... dead. Been gone for nine years,' she said, feeling a little ashamed of her lie.

'Oh, I'm sorry,' said Lawrence, his hand pausing on the already dry plate he was circling the dishcloth on.

'I have to tell that ...'

'No need to explain, I understand.' The hand continued, a little faster now, almost musically, and an unexpected warmth crept up Mary's chest.

When the dishes were dried, Lawrence nodded to Mary

and headed up to his room.

'Hey, Lawrence, want to play a game?' Mary heard Marina call out as he walked past the lounge.

'Don't bother Lawrence!' called Mary, still in the kitchen.

He peeped back in, his eyebrows raised in question.

'Of course, if you really want to.' Mary shrugged and snickered. 'Your funeral. Marina is the champ.'

He winked at her and went into the lounge. Mary put her hands on the back of the kitchen chair and smiled. Then once she had put away all the dishes and the kitchen was tidy, she went in to join them. She admired the ease with which he talked with the couple and the same ease with which he chatted with the girls. She resisted requests for her to join the game, preferring to watch them all pretend to be a family, wishing it were real, that this was what she should have had.

'Another game?' asked Lucille, her eyes widening in hope when the game was finished. She had been gawking at Lawrence the whole time, but still managed to focus on the game, even winning and poking her tongue out at a sour Marina.

'These games take forever,' said Mary. 'I think that's enough for today.' She could see the Davises wanted to settle down with their selection of videos they had hired when they went for a stroll in the afternoon.

'Can we stay in the lounge and read?' Lucille clasped her hands together. 'Just for a little while, Mum?'

Mary looked at the clock. It was still early, just past eight p.m., and she was feeling light, pleasant, which was helped by the patter of the non-stop rain on the windowpane. 'Okay, just for half an hour,' she said.

'One hour?' asked Marina.

'Half an hour,' said Mary, creasing her eyes, and the girls scampered off to their room, each returning with a book.

'Not a great evening for a walk,' said Lawrence, and Mary was thrilled with the twinge of disappointment in his voice.

'No,' said Mary regretfully. 'Perhaps next time.'

'I won't see you tomorrow. I will be leaving pretty early again,' he said when he was about to head up the stairs.

'You know where to leave the key,' replied Mary, hoping her own disappointment was well hidden.

'Thank you for the lovely accommodation.'

'Well,' said Mary looking about her. 'It's not much, but …'

'It's the best I've been to,' he said and lightly touched her hand that rested on the banister.

Her hand recoiled as if it had been burnt and she saw a small frown appear on his face. She swallowed. 'We've loved having you,' she said. 'Me and the girls.' She fled to the porch.

CHAPTER 5

Mary almost wished Lawrence had never stopped into her boarding house that first night, the way her thoughts kept returning to him, unnerving her. She didn't know when and if he would return and she knew she had hurt him when she withdrew her hand from his. The rebuff may have turned him off for good. How much could a man show interest in a woman when all she did was play it cool? Then she shook free thoughts of him, berating herself for even thinking those thoughts that were a deception to the memory of her husband. But they weren't lustful thoughts, she managed to keep those at bay. She had just enjoyed his company, even though she knew she was not prone to enjoying the company of someone so much younger, especially that of a man. But he didn't act or speak like a young man, he seemed older, like an old-fashioned gentleman, a young Clark Gable, albeit a little less confident. But it was just his downright gentleness that unnerved her, the way he talked in that low voice. Not about himself, never about himself; she in fact knew very little about him. But he listened, was interested in the mundane things, which was her life, the weather, the boarding house, the beach, her girls. Gary would have loved this guy.

But it had been nearly three weeks and she had all but given up hope ...

'Hey, Mary-Louise.' Mary's thoughts were interrupted by the grating sound of Virginia's voice from the reception room, and she winced. Virginia was still a busybody, sticking her nose in everyone's business. The perfect husband, two perfect teenage girls and a perfect blue weatherboard house that announced to the few visitors to Righteous Creek that they were entering a beach haven with a perfect population. She had moved on from her infatuation with Gary once she realised she was not going to tear him away from Mary, and hooked up with Chester, a professional football player, less than a month later, and had married him. But she had never forgiven Mary for wooing away the man, who she insisted had his eyes on her first. Mary knew better than to argue; she had learned that early in life, not just with her parents, but with kids at school, people on the street. But once she realised how Gary won over the hearts and minds of the people of the Creek, Virginia reluctantly accepted that things had changed.

For the while she was Gary's wife, Mary let the gossips eat their words, kept her head high as she always had, tried to ignore the now sweet calls from across the street in the same way she'd previously ignored their cruel snipes. Then Gary died, and they all reverted to type. The invitations she'd received for weddings, dances, birthday parties all stopped. Even the parents of the friends of her children stopped inviting them on play dates, and Mary thought it curious that she was in fact a little relieved. Keeping up the farce of a Stepford Wife was tiring. Although Gary thrived on their social life, she found it hard to fake interest in the lives of people who she knew were only her friends because of her husband, and she knew Virginia had played a big part in the way people treated her again.

But here was Virginia, the only person who still called her by her full name, a name she despised, a fact Virginia was well aware of. 'Hello, Virgie,' she called back from the kitchen, feeling a little thrill at getting a little of her own back. 'I'm in the kitchen.' *What does she want?* thought Mary. Virginia only came to the boarding house when she needed something, a place to put up visitors, and a place to leave her well-behaved children when she needed time with her husband. And Mary knew what that meant. She had seen women who had come in from the cold, battered and bruised, those who were willing to share their story and those who covered their faces in foundation so thick, they looked like the icing on the cake she baked for her girls' birthdays.

Virginia stepped into the kitchen, dark sunglasses covering her eyes, and Mary glanced out of the window to reassure herself that the sun was indeed still hidden. It had been a gloomy few days, bringing with it a depressing atmosphere in the middle of spring. It was almost dark outside, even though it was only six in the evening. Mary smiled at Virginia encouragingly. Even though she could never trust her, she felt a sliver of sympathy. She had learned not to judge people until she had been in their shoes. Life had taught her that.

'I ... erm, I need a favour.'

'Sure. Do you have someone who needs a place?'

'Yes.' Virginia took off her glasses and shifted her weight to her other high-heeled foot. Mary looked back into the sink, trying not to show her reaction to the sheen of yellow on the corner of Virginia's left eye. Virginia quickly put her glasses back on. 'Well, no,' she said unsurely. 'I was hoping that ...'

Mary didn't know why but she wanted to relieve this woman of having to explain herself. 'You need me to watch the girls?'

Virginia's chest fell in relief and a little cry left her

mouth. 'Just for the night.'

'Not a problem. They've stayed before so they know the layout. Besides, Lucille and Marina will be happy to have company.'

Even through the dark glasses, she saw the frown appear on Virginia's face and Mary clenched her teeth and gripped the side of the sink. The nerve of the woman. Her kids were too good for Mary's? But she didn't think they were too good for her boarding house! 'Yes, yes,' said Virginia hurriedly, clearly perceiving Mary's change in demeanour. 'They would like that.'

Mary knew that already. The few times she had left her girls for Mary to watch, they had all had a ball. They turned up the music and danced and sang, entertaining the Davises and other guests that had been there. 'What time?' she said curtly.

'Erm … they're in the car.'

Mary smiled despite herself. Everyone knew she was a softie. They may not give her the time of day, but they were always ready to take her help. Even with the work required for the boarding house and with her sewing—sure, a task she loved—she volunteered once a week, driving lunches to the elderly. Maybe it was the company, as she stopped in sometimes to chat with the senior men and women, mostly lonely single people who had lost their spouses, and were in need of a kind ear. She sometimes wondered if she did it for her own selfish reasons, to seek the care of the parents who never gave her any.

And here was Virginia, as usual taking advantage of her generosity, not even considering how she had treated her in their youth and even beyond. But Mary wanted to let the past be just that. Apart from her constants reminisces about Gary, she preferred not to let what was done and dusted be a part of her life anymore. She wondered what Virginia was going to do, but stopped herself. She had heard people talking already about the marriage that was on the rocks. But what Virginia did was not her business; she refused to be drawn into the gossipy antics of the town. They had shown her where she really stood the day Gary had died. Besides, it was terribly unfair when there were children involved. She knew well what gossip could do.

Virginia didn't come back the next day. She called and asked if the girls could stay a little longer and as it was the tail end of the school holidays, Mary obliged. Desiree and Paulette were having the time of their lives; just a little younger than Mary's own girls, they were delightful. Mary leaned in the doorway and watched as they played in the games room with Lucille and Marina and wondered if she was supposed to do anything with them, like make them complete their holiday homework. But she shrugged. They were left in her care and Virginia hadn't left any instructions. Let them have some fun when they could.

The rain subsided by midday the next day, and the sun shone so brightly that Mary let the children go for a swim, watching them from the porch. She sat on the step, sipping iced water, and for a second, felt a sense of freedom. She raised her skirt to just above her knees and tilted her head back, her eyes closed, feeling the warmth fill the pores on her face. She wished Gary were beside her. For the two years they spent together in this place, they loved just this, basking in the sun, their arms and legs tangled with each other, not knowing whose was whose, and when it got too hot, they'd go for a dip. And something about the effort, something about the sun, something about the water, would leave them hungry for each other, and they would dash to the bedroom, scrambling to get their clothes off, sometimes not waiting to, and make love. Then they would laugh at each other, come down from the bedroom and hope that no one had noticed their careless lust. They would make iced tea and sit back on the porch, daring each other for more.

Oh Gary, she cried inwardly.

'Ahem.'

Mary's eyes darted open as a shadow loomed over her. She shielded her eyes to acclimatise them to the light and quickly pulled down her skirt to cover her legs, realising it was Lawrence who stood before her. A knot stuck in her throat and she looked back up at him. A smile skirted his lips and Mary blushed. He held out his hand to help her up, but she pretended not to notice and raised herself without his assistance. Lawrence!

'Hello,' she managed.

'Hello, Mary.' His voice was low, gentle.

She noticed his suitcase and felt her heart knock hard at her chest. She only now realised how much she really wanted him to return. 'Business trip again?' She straightened her dress and patted her mussed hair, the long plait unruly from the humidity of the sea air.

'Actually, no,' he said and looked towards the ocean. Mary followed his gaze and smiled at the girls still frolicking on the sand, only Lucille in the water, the waves just above her waist. Lucille was a strong swimmer, but she still worried about leaving them all alone in the sea and she frowned.

'The girls have some company?'

'Yes,' she said, nodding. 'A friend ...' She nearly baulked at the word. 'A friend's kids. Just keeping an eye on them for a couple of days.' Mary suddenly realised what he had said. 'You're not here on business?'

'I had a week off, so I thought I'd drive down to my favourite beachside town.' He smiled and then pursed his lips. 'Do you have room?'

'Yes, yes, of course.' There were only a couple of times that the boarding house had been full. The first had been a couple of years ago when the Aircraft Expo came to Palermo Haven, a resort town four kilometres down the road, and last year, when Hattie, the socialite, much more arrogant and hoity than Virginia, had gotten married, and they had to squeeze in boarders from everywhere, much to the disdain of the Davises, who were quite put out about their home being invaded by prissy, spoilt, nose-waving strangers.

With another glance towards the water, she headed up the stairs, motioning for him to follow.

'If it's the same room, I can find my way,' he said, sensing her hesitance to leave the girls near the water on their own.

Of course his room was empty. She'd made sure that it would be the last to be rented, on the off chance that he returned. Besides, it was the one above her own and she liked the thought of him being so close. 'Yes, same room,' she said. 'Do you know where the key is?'

He nodded and went inside, and Mary was a little embarrassed that she looked like an overbearing mother, unable to leave her daughters alone for a moment. But she couldn't risk anything happening to them. She couldn't afford more misery. She would not survive.

CHAPTER 6

'How about that walk?'

Mary was standing on the porch, looking out into the dark ocean, her hands resting on the banister. She gripped it tighter and didn't turn around immediately. She had been expecting him to remind her of her promise to him the last time he was here. She gave a small nod and pulled her shawl around her shoulders, stepping down the path, and Lawrence fell in step with her.

'Where are the girls?' Lawrence asked.

'They're watching movies with Mr and Mrs Davis.' She snickered.

'Why the laugh?' he asked.

'Well, since we got the video player, the Davises have taken it upon themselves to introduce the girls to the old movies, you know, the golden age of cinema.'

'And do they enjoy it?'

'I think they do actually.' She chuckled again. 'They all walk to the video rental place, a mighty walk from here, almost a kilometre. Then they negotiate. Five movies, three chosen by the Davises and two by the girls. The deal is they have to watch them together. That way they expand their film repertoire.'

Lawrence tutted. 'That's a pretty good deal.'

'I don't know about today though. They have the girls watching *The Birds*.'

'Wow, that's a doozy.'

'Lucille will love it, but Marina, well …'

'She doesn't like Hitchcock?'

'Hmmm, I don't know. I never know when something will affect her, you know?' Mary turned to look at Lawrence's face and found him frowning. 'Are you okay?'

'Yes,' he said and blinked hard. 'I was just wondering about that woman, your friend.' Mary knew he was changing the subject and wondered why.

'What about her?' Virginia had picked up the girls about an hour before and had bumped into Lawrence on the way in. She had stood there frozen, her mouth agape, her eyes glued to his face, and something about the way she looked at him reminded her of the way she had stared at Gary.

'Is she a close friend?'

'Why?'

'Just wondering.'

'Do you know her?' Mary's heart gave a loud clap of denial.

'No.' Lawrence didn't elaborate and Mary didn't persist.

They walked in silence for a few minutes, the sounds of

the people on the beach obscuring their thoughts, and they didn't realise it when they had moved past the clumps of beachgoers. The sky was a deep purple now and they had walked past the streetlamps into the dark of the tapering shore. Soon they would hit the rocks and would have to turn back. Mary didn't want to yet, she was enjoying this walk, the walk she usually made alone. Sometimes the girls would accompany her, but lately they were becoming their own people, preferring to do their own things, reading, hanging with their friends, but Marina ... They were growing up too soon.

'This is a lovely spot,' said Lawrence, interrupting Mary's thoughts.

He was looking out to sea, one leg hitched up on a rock, and Mary swallowed. He looked like something out of a romance novel, wisps of his hair blowing in the breeze, his profile stark against the evening sky. She walked past him to the edge of the water and felt the salty air cool her prickly cheeks. A flash of courage hit her. She needed to know.

'How old are you, Lawrence?'

There was no answer, but she could hear him shift behind her. 'Is it important?' His voice was so low and so close to her ear, she started. Without turning to him, she began to walk back from where they came.

'I think so,' she said finally, knowing it was.

'I'm twenty-nine.'

'I'm thirty-nine,' she replied, still walking.

They were silent the rest of the way home, and when they got to the house, Lawrence moved to the side, from which he could access his room. 'Goodnight, Mary.'

'Have a good night, Lawrence,' she replied curtly and went into the house. She stopped at the den, and watched the little group, Lucille, pretending to read while her eyes fluttered to the TV and back to her book. She smiled at Marina, who was sitting beside Mrs Davis, clutching at her blanket, her eyes wide in excitement. The Davises were sitting there, hand in hand, satisfied smirks on their faces. They always ribbed the girls when they liked a movie they had chosen. Mary tiptoed in and sat on the stool behind them, settling in to watch the rest of the movie with them.

CHAPTER 7

'This is stupid,' cried Marina. 'I don't want to go. It's a stupid party with stupid people and stupid music.'

'Yes, I know it's all very stupid,' replied Mary. Marina was acting more like a five-year-old than the teenager she was. 'But you haven't been to a party in so long. Jenny even came to the house to ask for you.'

'Leave her alone, Mum,' said Lucille, who was at the dining table studying for exams. 'She's right, they are stupid.'

'You're no help,' said Mary. She couldn't understand why her younger daughter had become so introverted and couldn't put her finger on when it happened.

The sound of the piano in the hallway suddenly tinkled and Mary froze. No one played it; in fact, no one even noticed it, it was so well hidden in the little alcove behind the stairs. Even Mrs Davis, who taught her how to play, didn't go near it when Mary was around. She knew the old woman played, could see the change in the placement of the seat, the fingerprints when she hadn't dusted on it, and she didn't mind at all. She just preferred not to hear it. Now her heart felt like it was falling out of her chest and her throat caught.

'Are you okay, Mum?' Lucille was looking at her in

concern.

Mary nodded and walked out of the house. She moved in quick, large strides to the edge of the water and kicked at the sand, her mind going to Gary again. His fingers on the piano, playing in tune with hers. At times he would jumble her rhythm and she would push him away playfully. The songs they would sing together, and when the girls were able, the four of them belting out tunes, and other boarders coming to join in their reverie. The piano was in the lounge then, taking pride of place, a centrepiece, a cornerstone of their joy. And then it wasn't. It was a painful reminder of what they were, what she had lost, of her loneliness, her despair.

She suddenly remembered she was in the middle of cooking and the stove was still on. How long had she been standing out here? She bolted back into the kitchen and found Lawrence at the stove, Marina by his side, stirring the casserole in the large pot.

'I'm sorry,' she said.

'All under control,' he replied, not turning around. 'It's nearly done, I think.'

'Thank you, I'll take over.'

'I'd rather do this than go to that stupid party,' said Marina, gesturing to the pot.

'How about I take you?' said Lawrence. 'I could drop you off and pick you up.' Marina stopped stirring for a second and propped her elbow on the counter. Lawrence leaned down and whispered, 'It will make your mum happy. And me too.'

Marina was a stubborn child, so when she let her mouth break out in a slow smile, Mary almost fell backwards. 'Okay, but just for an hour. I'll get ready.' She handed him the wooden spoon and as she walked past Mary, she rolled her eyes, but with a smile on her lips.

'Wow, how did you manage that?'

'Just the way I am,' he replied with a teasing smile. He handed Mary the spoon. 'Here you go, I don't know what sort of mess I've made with this.'

'I'm sure you managed fine.' Mary took the spoon from him and hoped he would leave. He didn't.

'The piano,' he said, apologetically. 'I didn't know. Lucille told me that no one plays it when you're around.'

Mary waved her hand. 'Oh, anyone can play it. It just came out of the blue, that's all.'

'Well, I'm sorry.'

'No, don't be. There're just some things …' She couldn't complete the sentence. How could she explain to someone the utter desolation she felt when she heard it played?

'I'd better go wait for Marina,' said Lawrence. 'You didn't mind that I offered to take her?'

'Of course not, and thank you again.' And when he turned to leave, she watched as he walked away, his shoulders straight, yet she could see he had his own demons, his own past, and was worried about how much she wanted to know about it. But that wouldn't do. For one, he was too young to be anything but a friend, and the guilt she felt when she thought about him was harder to bear.

CHAPTER 8

Mary avoided Lawrence as much as she could that week. She couldn't afford to fall for this man, who would inevitably leave her. Why would he be attracted to someone so much older than him? Maybe he just needed some female company and thought her an easy target, a lonely old widow, with not many options. But she didn't see that in the way he looked at her, as if he were searching her soul for something, but what that something was, she didn't know. Maybe a part of him that was missing that he thought he saw in her?

No. She shut her eyes tightly. How could she even be thinking about a relationship with this man? She couldn't have her children become attached to him as more than a boarder, a fun guy who popped in every now and again, had dinner and played board games with them. Besides, she was getting ahead of herself; he probably had no other intention with her than a nice place to stay and some company. He appeared lonely, a solitary soul, with much on his mind. Sometimes when she looked up from whatever she was doing, she could feel his eyes on her, and a few times when she dared to return his gaze, he looked away in embarrassment. He seemed to sense her discomfort and often she would find him walking the beach by himself, or sitting up on the balcony, a faraway expression on his face, looking beyond the sea or up to the stars. In those unguarded moments, Mary unintentionally studied him, a feeling of warmth coursing through her stomach, and at times, she held on to the feeling, letting it encompass her, a feeling she knew well and missed so much. She thought that perhaps it was the fact that she remembered what it felt like so well, a craving for love and heat and belonging, and as much as she tried to dismiss the thought, she saw he could give her all the things she needed and missed.

'Why doesn't Lawrence play games with us anymore?' Lucille asked one evening after Lawrence had retired to his room for the evening. Mary worried about her daughter. She was becoming more enamoured with him, and although Mary knew it was a teenage crush, and Lucille had already had a couple of those before, she didn't want to encourage her daughter's attraction to someone so much older than her.

'He's got his own life, Lucille,' said Mary.

Lucille pouted and Mary noticed the gloss that shone on her lips. Her daughter had prettied herself for Lawrence. 'But he didn't come down yesterday either.'

'He has work to do, I'm sure.'

'But he doesn't,' she insisted. 'He said he was here on a holiday.'

Mary didn't know how to respond so she shrugged.

Lucille took her mother's gesture as an invitation. 'Can I ask him to come down?' She put down her cards and pushed to the edge of her seat.

'I'll ask him tomorrow. He's probably already gone to bed.'

Lucille pouted again. 'I'm going to bed too,' she said.

'Hey, what about the game?' Marina shouted indignantly.

'I'm sick of playing games,' huffed Lucille and stomped off to her room. 'I'm sick of baby stuff.'

Marina rolled her eyes and turned to her mother, a desperate invitation to take Lucille's place. Mary smiled and sat opposite Marina, picking up a hand of cards. She needed to take the chance to communicate with her younger daughter whenever she could. Marina was getting way too touchy, too moody and rarely offered to spend time with her mother.

'So tell me, Marina, how was the party? You haven't said much since then.'

'It was what I thought it would be. Boring girls, gossiping about other girls and talking about boys.'

Mary was encouraged. Marina hadn't said more than a sentence to her in, well, she couldn't remember how long. 'Were your friends there? Were there boys?'

'Can we not talk about this anymore?'

'Sure, okay. What do you want to talk about?'

'Nothing. I want to play the game.'

Mary tried not to let her heart hurt. She looked up at the Davises, and Sylvia gave her a sympathetic smile. She smiled back at her and tried to be grateful that she had her children with her, that she was doing the best for them. She hoped Marina would grow out of whatever stage she was going through soon. The game ended quickly and Marina announced she was going to her room too.

'You're doing great, Mary,' said Sylvia when Mary leaned back on the sofa in despondency.

Mary smiled at the woman wanly. 'I'm trying, Mrs Davis. I just don't know what to do to get through to her.'

Mrs Davis edged closer to Mary and took her hand. 'She's at a tough stage, you know. I know we didn't have any children, but I saw many come through my doors. Each one had a difference about them and why they chose to play the piano.'

Mary stiffened. Mrs Davis had tried to talk her into playing again for a long time after Gary's death, but her attempts had been met with deference, annoyance and sometimes anger. She even remembered yelling at Mrs Davis to mind her own business once, a reaction she immediately regretted. Mrs Davis had not brought it up again and she hoped she wouldn't now.

'And I know why you did. You were gifted, there was no doubt, the moment you walked into my door.' Mary remembered it well, the day she finally had the guts to knock on the door at the age of fifteen, having saved three dollars from running errands for the neighbourhood, and ask if it was enough for lessons. The woman took one look at her, and gave her lessons twice a week for free, and asked her to come in to practise on her own whenever she liked, when the piano was not in use by other students.

'That's all in the past,' said Mary.

'I'm not trying to tell you to play, Mary. You will come back to that when your time is right.' She squeezed her shoulder and Mary felt a rush of warmth for this woman. 'What I'm trying to say is that I saw a lost little girl who grew up before my eyes into a beautiful, strong young woman. Someone who wasn't shown their worth.'

Mary was uncomfortable now. She'd never complained about the state of her homelife to Mrs Davis, but the woman had clearly guessed the love that was missing in her life. 'I was okay.'

'Yes, you were. And that's because of you. And you've turned into someone who, despite missing out on so much, is loving, kind, generous. What you've done for us …'

'Oh, Mrs Davis!' She grabbed the old woman's hands and held them tightly between her own. 'What you've done for me, what you both have done. I don't know if I could understand what love was supposed to be until I met you. I can never repay that, not till the day I die.' Mary was taken aback by her passion and Mrs Davis let a tear slip out of the corner of her eye.

'No, my dear. You became the child we couldn't have, and you don't understand what you have done for us. Not just letting us stay here for practically peanuts.' She extracted her hands from Mary's, pulling her close, and Mary again felt what it would be like in a mother's embrace. Mrs Davis leaned back. 'I've forgotten my point,' she said and chortled. 'Oh yes. My point was Marina. And Lucille. I see you as a mother and it makes my heart full. You didn't have what you should have had as a child, but you have given everything to these girls. Marina will grow out of whatever she is going through. Being a teenager is tough, especially in today's world, where everything is about freedom and free love and talking back to your parents.' She raised her eyebrows and gave a short laugh. 'She will be okay; I know they both will.'

'I hope you're right. I worry about both of them so much.'

'We are here too, you know,' said Mrs Davis.

'I know, and I can't imagine it if you hadn't come to live

with us.'

'Go on, child. Go find that handsome man to talk to.'

Mary blushed. 'Stop it, Mrs Davis. He's a young man and I'm …'

'A beautiful, sexy young woman.'

Mary smiled and kissed Mrs Davis on the cheek before going to the front porch where the moon was shaded behind a cloud, displaying a bleak ocean, little ripples of water running over its surface. Marina would be okay, as Mrs Davis had said, but she felt a tug at her heart. How could she be so sure about that? She was going more and more into herself lately and Mary wished she had more friends, more people that came to see her, as Lucille did. Lucille often had her two best friends in the house and they frolicked on the beach together. Marina used to go with them but hadn't in more than a couple of years, even though Lucille tried to cajole her into joining them. But now even Lucille couldn't persuade the hard-headed Marina into anything she didn't want to do.

At least Lucille didn't go through this stage. Sure, she had a stage of rebellion, where voices were loud and doors were slammed, but Lucille talked to Mary. She was a social being that thrived on company. Just like her father. A shiver of fear ran up Mary's spine. She hoped not quite like her father, who kept his demons buried so deep, even Mary didn't know they existed until it was too late.

But she would have to keep an eye on her eldest daughter. She was beginning to go out more often than Mary liked, and with people Mary didn't know too well. She knew it was the age; she would be eighteen soon, and every eighteen-year-old was a pain in their parents' temple. She remembered being eighteen all too well, but then again, she was always a pain in her parents' lives, an intrusion into their world.

But there were already boys, some that lurked by their house, outside on the beach. The tall, ginger-haired surfie, who was way too old to be flirting with a seventeen-year-old. Mary had stood at the door, a broom in her hand, and stared directly at the young lad, who at first tried to stare back in defiance and then realised that Mary was not one to be trifled with. Then just last week, a boy more her age, who just kept walking past the house, up and down, up and down …

She could see the attraction; her daughter was more than attractive, dark flowing locks, piercing grey eyes which she got from Gary, and that chin, which she jutted out, accentuating her full lips. She would have to stock up on brooms, she'd realised that quite early on. She tried to talk to Lucille about it all last year, but her daughter gasped in indignation.

'Mum, they teach us stuff at school!'

'Do they?' Mary didn't remember learning anything of life's necessities at school. 'What do they teach you?'

'Well,' Lucille sounded unsure now. 'You know, the birds and the bees, and all that.'

'But how about how to handle, you know, the opposite sex?'

'Mum! Don't speak like that!'

Mary knew she needed to educate her daughter on sex. If Lucille was taught what Mary had been taught, then it was next to nothing. She learned for herself, the drunken bouts of sex her parents had, the noise so loud she had to cover her ears in the next room. Her mother confiding in her one drunken evening, when Mary was just eleven years old, the number of abortions she'd had to endure. And the last straw: her mother giving birth to a sister who was so small she died at two months—she never even made it home from the hospital—and that was when Mary knew her parents were selfish louts who had no time for anyone but themselves, and of course alcohol.

'Come on, we're taking a walk,' she said. She left Marina with the Davises and told a very embarrassed Lucille about how to protect herself from boys and pregnancy.

Mary just hoped she had taught her what she needed to learn before she was faced with anything, but she still chuckled when the boys casually strolled past, their heads darting towards the house. So far Lucille had not seemed interested in any of them, save for Peter, the shy boy who she had met on the beach last summer. And when he left to go back from where he came—Melbourne—Lucille lounged on the steps of the porch for days, staring into the ocean, her lips pursed, her eyes drooping. Then came Kyle and she was soon back to herself.

But this interest in Lawrence, Mary could not encourage. Lucille was at an impressionable age and teenagers thought they were in love all the time. Mary remembered her own infatuation with a boy called Davy in high school, a boy who tried to court her many times. But she knew, even then, the ones not to let get too close. She based all her choices in men on her father, or more like, the opposite of her father.

And when Gary had come into her life, a man who, after the recital, visited the café at which she worked on his way through town, she knew she could give it all to him. And she did. And he left; no, he died. And she resented him for that more than if he'd left.

CHAPTER 9

It was in the third week in the summer of '72 when Mary realised it was too late. She had already fallen in love with Lawrence. A man she'd met less than six months before, a man who she tried to avoid when he came through town and stayed at the boarding house. A man who didn't take her nonchalance for rejection, but kept coming, hoping there was room at Jesse's Boarding for him, always trying to hide his beaming smile with his long fingers when she welcomed him back with warmth.

It was a hot summer, the lingering of winter barely leaving time to spring to adjust when the long, hot days took over. And this year, there was an influx of reservations, so much so that when Sophie called to book a room, something she never really did, always assuming there would be space, Mary was flustered. Sophie was on a break from filming a movie, which was going to be a blockbuster. A bit role, but she had lines, four of them, and this was going to be her big break. She needed a place to unwind before she started shooting.

'Of course, there's room for you. I always have a room for you.'

'Well, I don't know anymore. I haven't been there in months. Maybe you found some rich man and left me.'

Mary laughed. She loved Sophie's way with words.

Sophie, who was always teasing her, but who she knew she could trust with her life. 'Yes, Sophie. Rich men are my thing. I hunt them out and ensnare them.'

'Well, I would if I were you,' sniffed Sophie. 'Is today okay?'

'Yes, it's a little busy this week, so you may have to deal with other people.'

'Great! That's my beach. Tell them all to leave. I want you to myself.'

'How long will you be staying?'

'Two weeks of leisure before I go back to the pit,' she said with mirth.

'I'll set it up for you.' Mary hung up and put her chin in her hands.

Lawrence's room was always kept free, and the rest of the rooms were booked, but she couldn't let Sophie down. Sophie had never let her down, she was the closest thing to a friend Mary had. So she did it, she gave her Lawrence's room, praying that Lawrence would not show up unexpectedly, as he always did.

Sophie rolled through the door at six p.m. with a flourish, and the girls, who were fond of 'Aunt' Sophie, rushed to her, Lucille encasing her in her arms, swaying along with her. Marina stood by and waited for Sophie to hug her after Lucille had finally let go.

'You're nearly taller than me,' she exclaimed after releasing Marina from her grip. 'How long has it been, and what are you feeding them?' she asked Mary who watched the scene with warmth.

'Are you going to eat with us?' asked Lucille.

'Yes, of course I am, if your mother has had the heart to think of me!'

'Nah, you can sit and watch us, and eat your heart out,' Mary teased. 'I've cooked your favourite. Pork roast, and apple pie for dessert.'

'No,' groaned Sophie. 'I have a part to prepare for. How could you do this to me?'

'Well, you will have to get off your silly diet for one night.'

'Come and hug me, woman,' said Sophie and enfolded Mary in her arms. Mary squeezed Sophie tight, wishing she could stay more than the promised two weeks.

'Come on, ladies,' Sophie said to the girls who were hanging around. 'Let's see what I have in my bag for you.'

'You really shouldn't bring them things every time you come,' admonished Mary.

'Why not?' said Sophie. 'I love these two better than my own nieces, those ungrateful rascals.' She turned to the rooms. 'Where am I staying today?'

'I'll take you,' said Lucille and took her suitcase, Marina grabbing her carpet bag.

'I have to set up for dinner,' said Mary. 'Twenty minutes.'

Today Mary decided to eat with the rest of the guests

who had chosen to eat at the boarding house. She wanted to chat with Sophie about her life since she'd last seen her and hear of her usual tales of adventure. She didn't disappoint, telling them of a tall, dark and handsome man that she had met who turned out to be a swindler and how she had caught him red-handed in her sock drawer, where she kept her blue velvet bag of jewellery.

'And he looked at me as if I was the one who was doing the wrong thing!'

'What did you do?' asked Lucille, her eyes wide with excitement.

'What could I do? I grabbed the closest thing to me, the lamp, and I threw it at his head!' The whole table was silent, listening in captivation, their cutlery, in various poses, unmoving.

'And then?'

'I think I got his ear, but he shrieked like a little old woman!' She turned her head across the fascinated faces. 'So I grabbed him and pushed him out the door. And I found ...'

The bell on the front door clanged and Sophie stopped, irritated that someone had the gall to interrupt her story. Mary excused herself and when she got to the reception, she found Lawrence standing at the desk, a hopeful smile on his face. Her heart soared at the sight of him, racing as it usually did when he came here, and it dropped just as swiftly.

'Room for me?' he asked, his suitcase still in hand.

'Um ...'

She saw his smile turn to a slight frown, a disappointment that gathered his brows together. 'No, no,' she said quickly. She thought fast, her mind going to her emergency plan in case it ever came a time when there were too many guests, which she had not used often. 'But we have to do a little shuffling.' She could not turn Lawrence away. She just wished he would give her more notice, as a matter of practicality as well as time to calm the state of her nerves.

'Oh. I can come back when you're a little less full.' The regret in his voice was unmistakable.

'No, it's fine. We've done it before,' she said. 'The girls will stay with me.' The girls would have to stay in her room, the spare mattress from under her bed would have to be rolled out. This meant that Lawrence's room was right beside hers, but she couldn't think of that. It wasn't important. She still wondered why he kept returning when she had shown him no interest other than a few chats on the porch and their one walk along the beach. 'How long will you be staying?' asked Mary, grabbing the keys for the girls' room from the locked drawer.

'I can come another time, maybe when it's less busy,' he insisted apologetically. He seemed mortified that she was taking the girls' room from them. Mary was more pleased that he had said he'd come another time rather than looking for someplace else to stay.

'Hello, who is this?' Sophie was standing in the doorway.

'Sophie, this is Lawrence.'

'And this is the famous Sophie,' said Lawrence.

'Oh, you've heard of me,' said Sophie, sauntering up to him and holding out her hand.

'Yes, Mary has spoken of you with fondness.'

'Oh,' said Sophie with disappointment. 'Well, she has

never mentioned you,' she said, clearly rebuffed.

Lawrence's expression shifted slightly but Mary noticed and her heart had already fallen. With the gorgeous Sophie around, Lawrence would be less inclined to think she was important.

'I have to get the rooms ready,' she said.

'I'll help,' said Lawrence.

'No, really. There's a lot of food left over. You should grab some. Are you okay to do that?'

'That can wait,' he said. 'But are you sure …'

'The girls love it when I have them in with me. We stay up late and they take advantage of it, especially on holidays, so don't worry, you'll be doing them a favour.'

Lawrence didn't look convinced but helped her as she shuffled from one room to the other, making up the beds and moving clothes from the drawers, heaping them in Mary's own wardrobe, which had more than enough room for them. He didn't enter her bedroom, passing the girls' things between the rooms in the hallway.

'You need some help?' he called out, standing at the door and looking in the opposite direction as she struggled to pull the mattress out from under her bed.

'No,' she puffed out. 'I'm fine. Nearly got it.' She gave a mighty tug and landed on her backside. She looked up to see Lawrence trying not to laugh and burst out laughing herself. 'Okay, I need help,' she said and he came and knelt beside her.

'You should laugh more often,' he whispered, his

proximity unnerving her. 'It suits you.'

'How long are you staying?' she asked, sitting back on the floor, and looking straight into his eyes.

'I was thinking three weeks,' he said and she nodded, trying not to let her face break out into a smile, and reaching forward, they pulled out the mattress together.

CHAPTER 10

'That one's a looker,' said Sophie, her tapered legs on the porch rail, a cigarette dangling from her mouth. For a woman nearing forty, she could certainly pull stares from passers-by on the beach, her long red hair always in glamourous curls, a large pair of sunglasses aways covering her perfectly aligned eyes.

Mary, who was already looking at the long, tanned legs of Lawrence running into the water, blushed. He was wearing a thin blue t-shirt that stuck to his back and she could see the ripples from his shoulders and back muscles. 'Who?' She cleared her throat and Sophie chuckled.

'Don't play coy with me, lady. I've seen you stare at him.'

'I do not!' Mary turned her head to the other side so Sophie wouldn't see her cheeks darken with colour. She tried not to gaze at Lawrence overtly but Sophie was no fool.

Lawrence was splashing water over Marina, who was screaming wildly, and Mary envied the way he could get to her, like she hadn't been able to. Lucille stood at the edge of the water, one leg behind the other, her arms crossed, watching them play.

'Get in with the kids first, eh?' Sophie took a long drag of her cigarette and chuckled.

'It's not like that at all,' Mary insisted.

'I may be a self-obsessed wannabe, but I can still see, you know.'

'And what can you see?' As much as Mary was embarrassed, she still wanted to know what people really saw, an objective view of the situation.

'Oh stop it!' said Sophie. 'It's clear as day.'

'What is?'

'The way that man looks at you, at everything you do. Everyone around, including me, who usually can turn a head at the snap of my fingers'—she clicked her thumb and finger in example—'is invisible.'

'No, that's not it. You're seeing things,' replied Mary, a twist in her stomach.

'Come on, lady,' said Sophie. 'You may not have a face full of makeup as I do, or dress to the nines on any given day, but I would swap this glamour for a bit of that, what you have, I don't even know what to call it.' She wrinkled her nose in thought. 'Maybe that's why they call it *je ne sais quoi?*'

Mary didn't like attention, she never had, always veered away from it. Maybe that was why she didn't do anything outwardly to enhance the way she looked. The less people that noticed her, the better. But now she found that she wanted to be the person Lawrence looked at, not anyone else, just Lawrence. She'd even let her long hair loose today and tied the front of her shirt in a knot.

'What? What are you thinking?' Sophie was looking up at her, her hands shading her eyes from the sun.

'That you're crazy!' Mary picked up Sophie's empty glass. 'Refill?'

'Ugh, not if you're offering that insipid iced tea again.'

Mary laughed. She never took anything Sophie said personally. 'Well, unless you have something better, that's what you're getting.'

Sophie groaned again. 'Maybe I'll head up to Al's when it cools. Get some real stuff.'

Mary nodded. She didn't like to be near alcohol, but it wasn't like it was banned from the boarding house. Guests were free to do what they wanted to unless it turned unruly. She went in to prepare dinner. It was going to be a big chore and she wished Lucille would come in to help, but she was too busy making googly eyes at Lawrence. She wished she had already turned the place into a bed and breakfast, so she wouldn't have to deal with two meals, especially when it was a full house, but that also meant a cut in income, so she'd held off for a little longer. She was regretting it now.

She poured the iced tea into a long glass and looked out the window. It was darker in the house and so she could watch the goings-on outside, where the sun was shining bright, unobserved. Lawrence was standing knee deep in the water and he was in the process of removing his shirt. Mary turned away, begging her nerves to stop. It just wouldn't do to covet something she could, no, should, never have. She leaned back on the sink and lifted her head slowly to look at him again. In that moment he turned his head right around and even in the safety of the dark kitchen, she darted behind the curtain.

'Why not?' Sophie was standing at the door, her hand on her hip, knowing eyes defying her.

Mary sighed. 'Do you know how old he is? Or how young he is, more like it?'

'No, how young?'

Mary looked at the floor and chuckled. 'Twenty-nine.'

'Ha!' Sophie let out a loud laugh. 'So?'

'But you can see, Sophie,' she said, pointing towards the window. 'He is so much younger than me. Ten years!'

'Darling,' said Sophie, approaching the sink and taking the tea from Mary's hand. 'I sleep with many men half my age, most of the time, more.'

'Oh my gosh, I don't mean I want to ...' She laughed at Sophie's narrowed eyes. 'Yes, well ...'

'Well, nothing. Take it! I've known you for more than five years now. I've never seen you with a man, you've never talked about anyone but your precious Gary ...' She put up her hand in apology when she saw Mary's eyes narrow. 'I know, I know, he was the love of your life, there will never be another, and all that, but I can see you're lonely.'

'If you haven't noticed, I have two children to consider.'

'I'm sure they would like to see their mother happy.'

'Sure, but not with a man who is half my age ...' She ignored Sophie's rolling eyes. 'There are enough influences out there, free love and all that. They need some stability in their lives.'

'You can't keep trying to be what your parents were not. You are nothing like them. You turn your nose up at the mention of wine and I've never seen you raise your hand at your children, not even your voice.'

'Well, there's never been reason to. They are great kids.'

'Uh huh,' said Sophie, nodding. 'Because of you and what you've sacrificed for them.'

'And I don't want to confuse them, not now, when they are at that age.' She looked out the window again, seeing Lucille walking slowly up the shoreline. 'As it is, Lucille has a little crush on him.'

'I saw that too.'

'You just see everything, don't you?' said Mary and flicked the dishcloth at Sophie's arm.

'Yes, I do. And even if he isn't supposed to be the love of your life, I think he can turn you to mush. I think he can be the right guy for just now.'

Mary was silent. It was the first time she'd let herself think of Lawrence in that way, really feel there could be something more. Whenever he came unbidden to her mind, she shooed him away, not allowing herself to get drawn into even imagining him being anything more than the boarder he was, a paying guest.

'Come on,' said Sophie, taking her arm. 'Let's go catch some more of that eye candy. Then I will help you with dinner.'

CHAPTER 11

The moon was high and the music was blasting from a battery-operated radio placed on one of the outdoor tables. Mary, the girls and Sophie, along with some of the other guests, a young couple from Melbourne and a woman who was holidaying with her teenage daughter, sat on beach chairs around a fire, just a few metres from the front of the house. A blanket was thrown on the sand and the couple danced in the middle of it, the woman shaking her hips and hair wildly, the man twisting up and down, lost in the music of Neil Young, Dr. Hook and Elton John.

'I could give these young peckers a run for their money,' sulked Sophie.

'Why don't you?' asked Mary. Sophie often waltzed through the house, a glass of wine in her hand, shaking her hips to the music on the radio.

'Because I will put them to shame,' replied Sophie. 'And why should I do that? Besides, I don't have a partner and you won't dance with me.'

Mary laughed. No, as much as she unwittingly swayed to music, her body awakening at any rhythm, she never let herself go, never let her body control her mind.

'What about that strapping man? Where is he?'

Mary shrugged despite herself. Lawrence hadn't appeared at the little party even though the night was young and Mary looked towards the house a number of times, willing him to appear, hoping he was okay. He was especially quiet after dinner and excused himself to bed early. Mary assumed it was because he had spent a big day at the beach and was worn out from running around after Marina.

A thought struck her. Maybe she had been playing it too cool. Maybe he was offended, had had enough of being ignored. He'd been here nearly a week and she hadn't said much to him at all, staying out of his way after dinner in case he suggested going for a walk again. She got up and looked at Sophie, who gave her a knowing look.

'I got the girls,' Sophie said with a wink.

Mary mouthed a thank you and went in search of Lawrence. She didn't want to knock on his door, had no real good reason to, but she didn't have to. She peeked into the lounge and found him sitting with the Davises and she stopped at the door in surprise. He looked up at her and motioned for her to join them.

'That's not true,' Mrs Davis was saying. 'I think Redford is much sexier than Newman.' They had the video player on pause and were debating the looks of the dashing stars of *Butch Cassidy and the Sundance Kid*.

'What do you think?' Lawrence asked Mary, who had never really thought about it before. She just wanted to laugh at Lawrence who seemed somewhat comfortable situated in this strange conversation.

She approached the television and peered at it to get a

better look. 'Hmmm, I have to disagree, Mrs Davis. I think Mr Redford is quite handsome. But Mr Newman, well, he is swoon-worthy.'

'My dear,' said Mrs Davis, while Lawrence bit his lip to stop from laughing. 'I don't think you are quite equipped to judge.' Mary stiffened and Lawrence froze. Realising her gaffe, Mrs Davis reddened. 'I just mean that you are never going to see past that lovely man who sits on the mantel.'

Mary saw Lawrence's eyes move to the small black-and-white photograph of Gary. Her breath caught and she swallowed, lowering her eyelids. She couldn't think of a reply.

'I don't think that's good manners, Sylvia,' said Mr Davis softly, placing a hand on his wife's arm.

'I'm sorry, Mary.' Mrs Davis' voice softened. 'I just meant to say that apart from my old fella here, he was the most dashing man I had ever laid eyes on, even in that photograph.' She turned to her husband defensively. 'I wasn't being awful. I just was saying …'

'It's fine,' said Mary, feeling sorry for Mrs Davis who had the propensity to sometimes shoot off at the mouth. 'It's a wonderful compliment that I'm sure Gary would have loved to hear come from you, Mrs Davis. He adored you.' She tried to calm her thumping heart and kept her eyes off Lawrence.

'Thank you, my dear.' She nodded to her husband and Mary could see she was embarrassed by her words. She returned to the previous topic. 'And I still disagree. I think Mr Redford is what you kids say these days—hot!' She gave a little cackle and Mary chuckled.

'Anyway, now that I've stated my opinion, I just came in to check on everyone,' said Mary.

'We're fine,' said Mr Davis. 'Just introducing the oldies to the young fella here.'

Mary swallowed. Another reminder of Lawrence's youth. 'Well, when your movie is done, you're welcome to join us. The youngsters out there are giving us a run for our money, jiving up a storm out there.'

'Shall we show them how it's done?' said Lawrence and Mary turned to him in surprise.

'You dance?'

'Don't you?'

'Well, no. I mean, I did, I can …' she stammered. She wasn't sure she wanted to dance with him; it would be a slap in the face to Gary.

'Go on, you show them,' said Mrs Davis, a twinkle in her eye. She had given up trying to convince Mary to start dating again. Every attempt, just like with the piano, was met with a resolute refusal. She rose from her seat. 'Let's see you two. Come on, love,' she said to her husband. 'Mr Redford and Mr Newman can wait.'

Lawrence's smile was wide and teasing and Mary glowered at him. She didn't even know if she could dance with anyone. Sure, she sometimes found herself moving to the music that played on the radio, mimicking the steps Gary used to lead her around the dance floor. Sometimes she would even do a little shimmy, like she had seen on the music show on Saturday evening. But to dance in front of people … and with another man!

Lawrence was already by her side, his hand taking hers, and she followed him out the door, her nerves moving her forward. When they reached the party, where Fred and Ginger were settling into a slow sway to the sounds of Olivia Newton-John, Sophie turned to her, and her eyes lit up as they moved to Mary's hand clutched tightly by Lawrence's.

'New song,' said Sophie, springing up and changed the tape on the recorder. Diana Ross's voice blasted out and Sophie grabbed the hands of the girls, Marina not looking very enthused, but Lucille all for it. Sophie looked like she was a little over watching the dancing couple have the floor all to themselves.

Mary moved slowly at first, reserved, aware of her surroundings, aware of her behaviour around the girls, but with Lawrence still holding her hand, moving her about, she began to let some of her inhibitions fall away and soon she was moving along with him, unable to keep the smile off her face. She could see his eyes light up, surprised, pleased, and it propelled her to keep going. She tried not to think about anything, except what Sophie had said earlier, that she deserved some joy too, and was soon rolling herself under his arm, shaking her hips and laughing freely, something she could rarely do without guilt hitting her.

'Can I dance with Lawrence?' asked Lucille, tapping Mary on her arm.

'Yes, of course,' said Mary, stepping aside. She needed a break anyway to gather her thoughts and took a seat on the sand, a puffing Sophie joining her.

'All that smoking isn't good. My stamina isn't what it used to be,' she said as she collapsed beside Mary. She regarded Mary, who was watching Lawrence dance with her laughing daughter, swishing her around. Lucille's eyes were shining and soon, Marina was with them, Lawrence twirling them both at the same time. 'Was that fun?'

'Yep. It's been a while since I danced like that.'

'You should do it more often. It suits you to look so happy.'

The song stopped and Marina pulled at Lucille's arm and Lucille, pouting, took her inside. She probably wanted something to drink, Mary surmised, and didn't want to go in by herself. Mary smiled at the way Lucille still looked out for her sister, as reluctant as she seemed about it.

Lawrence looked back towards Mary and her heart thumped when he held out his hand with a sly smile.

'I can't,' she said.

'Come on,' he replied and even though she knew it was a slower song which meant he would be holding her more closely, she took his hand, not knowing what impelled her to do so.

He pulled her up and in one swift move, his arm was on the small of her back and her arms took their place as naturally as if she'd danced with him all her life. She moved her head to one side so she didn't have to look at his face, but she could feel his breath on her hair, the hardness of his shoulder, the clamminess of his hand. She closed her eyes for a moment and she was with Gary, moving slowly on the ground, her feet barely touching the sand. She was floating in the arms of her husband. Nothing had happened in the last nine years, nothing had changed. She felt her eyes well and pushed away from Lawrence.

'I'm dizzy,' she said and touched her temple.

'Me too,' he said and let her go.

She went back to where Sophie was and sat back down on the sand, watching with a heavy heart as Lawrence turned and went back inside the house.

'You're already in love with him,' Sophie leaned over and whispered.

'No,' said Mary simply.

'Maybe you were too close to the, erm, situation, but from where I was sitting ...'

'Stop it, Sophie,' said Mary sternly. Her head was still spinning, her skin tingling.

She glanced back at the house just as Lucille and Marina came out again. She looked at her watch; it was getting late now, past ten thirty, and Marina was already yawning. She was glad they hadn't seen her dance with Lawrence. How could she have been so impulsive, so foolish? She was angry with herself. She lived for the girls, and she had let herself be held by another man—what would they think?

'Goodnight, Sophie,' she said and got up. She needed to get the girls settled. Perhaps do a little reading with Marina, taking advantage of the good mood her daughter was in, even though she knew Marina would be out like a light.

CHAPTER 12

The night was still, apart from the crickets that made their presence known in the bushes beside the stairs. It had been a long summer, full of noise, full of life, and now it was gone, the chill of autumn upon them before the summer breeze had slinked away. So had most of the boarders. Lawrence had left too. He hadn't spent the full three weeks at the boarding house as he had first told Mary he would. In fact, it was only three days after that night at the beach when he came out of the house looking flustered, his bags packed and an envelope with payment in his hand.

'I have to go,' he said hurriedly. 'It's an emergency.'

'Is everything okay?' Mary asked. She had been still smarting over their dance in the moonlit night, barefooted on the sand, and she was taken aback, still trying to push past the awkwardness that had befallen both of them. He didn't even eat dinner with them on those evenings, letting Mary know he was going out to eat.

'Yes, a family thing.' He pushed the envelope in her hand. 'The whole three weeks' payment is in there,' he said and before she could protest, he shook his head. 'Also in there is my number at home. Please let me know if you need anything.' He hesitated. 'Or if you just want to talk, or whatever.'

Mary nodded dumbly, and he reached forward and lay a kiss on her cheek. Then he turned on his heel and strode to the carpark, and Mary watched from the window as his car drove away, her hand resting on the cheek which was still warm from his lips.

She absently touched it again now, wondering if he would return. It had been three months and he hadn't come back, hadn't called. She'd fingered the envelope with his number scribbled on it in a hurried hand so many times, it was beginning to fade. She'd even picked up the phone once and lost her nerve. What would she say to him? *'Oh Lawrence, please come back because I miss you so much'? 'What is keeping you so busy that you don't have time to stop over?"* No, she knew she couldn't do that. Maybe he finally had got some sense and realised it was best if he never came back. She felt a sorrow in the pit of her stomach when she thought that, but it was probably for the best.

And life returned to its usual busyness, Lucille beginning the twelfth grade, Marina, the tenth, and even though the only permanent boarders were the Davises, Mary very rarely had spare time on her hands. In the season where there was a lull, Mary focused on her sewing. She had to compensate for her lack of income and spent most afternoons in the sunroom making clothes for children and adults, accessories for babies, and even managed to sell some of her wares to the local stores in Geelong.

Sophie hadn't been back since Lawrence had been there, but she called regularly to check in on Mary and tell her of her travels and Mary couldn't wait for her friend to return. By the end of winter, more people began stopping in at the boarding house, mostly for a night or two, and even though she was relieved that there was a trickle of income, it also meant more work—more washing, more meals, more cleaning. But to Mary, it was a good distraction from her thoughts, which strayed to

Lawrence less often than before.

Virginia had been leaving her daughters at the boarding house frequently and Mary didn't mind. They were no trouble, but it also meant that one of the rooms was taken quite often. At first, Virginia didn't say much, sheepishly dropping in, the girls in tow, and disappeared for a night or two, knowing they were safe in Mary's care. And Mary, knowing Virginia's marriage was not on solid ground and had probably been that way for a while, didn't ask any questions, unwilling to be an intruder into someone else's life. She also knew Virginia would be mortified if anyone else in town were to find out what her situation was, which was why she left the girls with Mary and not their grandparents or any of the trillion friends Virginia had.

'If word got out,' she had said, leaving her sentence unfinished, her trembling hand shaking the glass of water she held. They were waiting for the girls to return from school and Mary had invited Virginia to the porch to wait with her. Virginia had seemed extra nervous this evening and Mary, although she didn't want to know the woman's business, was also empathetic enough to understand that Virginia needed someone to just sit with, maybe talk to, someone who wouldn't judge her. She put her hand on Virginia's, feeling a pity for this woman who had to fake her happiness for the sake of her image.

'Word will not get out by my mouth,' said Mary softly.

Virginia stuck her chin out and looked towards the water but Mary would see a pool of water in her eye. 'I can't let him leave, Mary.' Mary didn't reply. 'Chester can be harsh, but he can also be soft and tender.' She dropped her head, staring at the ground. 'But I haven't seen any of that for a while.' She looked at Mary now. 'But it's there. It will come back,' she continued, as if she were trying to convince herself of it.

'It will be okay, Virginia.'

Virginia shook her head. 'I don't know. I thought this round with Clara was like the others ...' She looked up, looking scared, like she'd just revealed what she didn't mean to. She sighed. 'It was Cecelia last year. You know, the barmaid?'

Mary nodded. She didn't know Cecilia well but the woman, with her black cascading hair and sparkling eyes, seemed to be a friendly, albeit gregarious lady, a smile on her face and a song in her voice for everyone, even Mary. 'I don't know her, like actually know her, but I know who she is.'

'It's not just Clara and Cecilia. There were others too. And he doesn't even hide it from me anymore.'

'Have you thought of leaving him?'

Virginia's necked snapped up. 'No! I will not!'

'Does he want to ...?'

'He's not getting a divorce from me. I won't allow it.' She thumped her fist on her lap. 'These are phases, I know. I've been there ...' She turned her eyes away from Mary.

'What do you mean?' For some unfathomable reason, Mary's skin prickled and she uncharacteristically wanted to know more.

'I just meant that ... you know ... I've been tempted too.' She sipped at her iced tea. She lowered her eyelids. 'There was Colin, not long ago. You remember Colin from high school. I had a thing with him then. Maybe it was a revenge fling, to get back at Chester, but he had his own family and I never saw him as more than a distraction anyway.' Mary wondered how much of what Virginia was telling her was really true. 'But this one, this

Clara.' She spat out the name. 'This one doesn't seem to be going away.'

Mary changed the subject. 'What about the kids?'

'What about them?' Virginia's eyes narrowed.

'I just meant, what do they know?'

'I know they are not stupid. But they are good kids.' Her eyes teared up again and Mary felt sorry for her. Virginia seemed to be in her own world most of the time but she did love her children. 'At least here, they don't have to be in the middle …' She sniffed, allowing the tear to fall and didn't bother to wipe it off her cheek.

'They are welcome here anytime.'

Virginia nodded. 'At least there's no drama here.' She attempted a laugh that petered out quickly.

'No,' said Mary with a chuckle. 'A boring little house with not much going on.'

'What about that man? Lawrence?'

Mary's skin prickled again. 'What about him?'

'He was cute.' Virginia smiled mischievously. 'Maybe when I've had enough of being left alone …'

To Mary's relief, she saw the girls approach on their walk back from the bus stop. 'They're back,' she said and stood up, waving at the foursome, three of them with their arms entwined, Marina following behind, a scowl on her face.

CHAPTER 13

Mary sat on the front step, smelling the sea breeze, salty, cool, and thought about her conversation with Virginia. She was glad she didn't have to go through all that drama anymore. Men, apart from Lawrence, who she was sure had had enough of her frigidity, had not been important to her, not since Gary, and not much before him either. And she was sure that in time, she could rid her mind of Lawrence. If he stayed away. But even now, a little part of her wished he would return.

'Mum,' Marina's voice called at the door.

'Yes, baby?' she replied, turning around to see her youngest daughter peeping out the screen door.

'Can I sit with you?'

'Come on,' she said. Mary worried for Marina. She was moving more and more into herself, the vivacious, carefree little girl had all but disappeared before her very eyes; she'd lost weight, her hair dragged in rat tails, and she very rarely came out of her room, even when the Davises tried to coax her out with a scary movie.

Mary put an arm around her as Marina sat on the step beside her. 'It's cold,' she said, feeling the spikes of goosebumps on her daughter's arm.

'I'm okay.' Marina snuggled her head on Mary's chest and Mary was surprised. It was unusual for Marina to show such affection of late.

They sat in silence, Mary rubbing Marina's arm up and down, and after a few minutes, Marina kissed her mother on the cheek. 'I'm going to bed now,' she said. Mary pulled her into a quick hug, which Marina tried to duck out of.

Mary felt slighted. It wasn't the first time her daughter had been distant but it was odd. She had just been sitting by her side with Mary's arm around her a moment ago, and now she didn't want to be hugged. Mary didn't quite know how to deal with it. When she asked Lucille about it, Lucille dismissed her mother's concern.

'She is being a teenager,' said Lucille. 'You complained at me too when I didn't want to talk to you all the time.'

'But you did talk to me,' Mary insisted. 'Even if you were angry or sad, or whatever you were feeling.'

'Everyone's different, Mum. It's high school. It's a bitch out there.'

'Lucille!'

'Oh Mum,' Lucille said, rolling her eyes, and she saw the frown on her mother's face. 'Okay, okay. I won't swear in front of you.'

'Hmph,' replied Mary. 'Can you talk to her?'

'I can try, but I can also tell you it's nothing.' She shrugged. 'Weren't you ever a teenager? Didn't you ever have teenage secrets?'

'Do you?' Mary turned her attention to Lucille.

Her daughter laughed. 'Nothing I can't handle,' she said.

Yes, Lucille was tough as nails, was focused on her studies, nursing it was, psychiatric nursing. She had always had an interest in it, and even though she didn't voice it, Mary knew it was the death of her father and his demons that drew her to it. Lucille wanted to understand it, and to care for the people like him; saving them was saving her father.

And even though she had a string of boys still loitering around the beach, Lucille didn't care for their glances as much as she used to. Now Mary had to focus her attention on Marina, try to make her tough too, but it was going to be a difficult task. Marina had always been more emotional, more highly strung, but always in a happy state. Now it seemed her lows could be just as extreme. Just like Gary.

Mary often wondered why she wasn't enough for Gary. Why he had taken his life. She thought about Marina who had just been leaning into the crook of her arm and very suddenly had left. Was it the same with her? Did she have the same demons Gary did?

She leaned her head on the wooden rail and her heart tugged at her again. 'Why, Gary?' she whispered, her chest so tight she felt it would explode. She tried to remember the last conversation she had with him. It was as she was leaving to take Lucille to school. 'Could you take out the bins before you shower?'

He had nodded and smiled broadly. Then as she was about to walk out the door, he reached out and gave her a hug.

'I'll be back in twenty minutes,' she said, laughing, but he pulled Lucille towards him as well and held her for a moment.

Such an insignificant interaction, but she should have noticed. Thinking back, she should have known. There were other things too, signs she saw, things she tried to talk to him about. The mood swings. He was never angry, never raised his voice to her once in all their time together, but there were times of darkness. She remembered the first time clearly. They had just come back from a dance, and Gary had been the centre of attention, as he always was. Mary loved that about him; it may not have been her thing, but she loved how he revelled in the attention. An officer, now stationed in Righteous Creek, he knew how to schmooze and Mary would sit at a table and watch with amusement as women threw themselves at him. She was never jealous, even encouraging him to dance with some of them when her feet were tired.

'I wouldn't hold another woman after I've had you in my arms,' he said.

'But I don't mind. I'm not the green-eyed type.'

'Why not?' he retorted.

'Do you want me to be?'

He cocked his head in thought. 'Maybe a little.'

'Why?'

'Well, because when men look at you, I want to tear their throats out.'

'Well, lucky they don't then,' she replied.

'You are an oblivious woman, aren't you?' He looked around the room with a frown. 'And I'm glad you are.' He pulled her out of her chair and spun her around in a lavish display across the dance floor and Mary had never been so happy in all her life.

But when they had gotten into the car, he became silent and although Mary tried to recount what had happened during the dance, he remained silent, his eyes steadfast on the road ahead. When he reached her house, he leaned over and kissed her lightly on the cheek. They had been on a few dates already, but Mary worried that this may have been the last one and half expected not to hear from him again. She wondered what she had done to upset him. He said he was jealous but she had eyes for no one but him. No one could ever make her feel the way he did and she spent the night in fear, hoping she hadn't done anything to lose him. But the next morning, he was at her door, telling her he was driving her to work, his face beaming, his eyes full of love. Mary forgot all about his mood the night before. But she saw more of it in time; it was hard to ignore when he became her husband.

She smiled now as she thought of how he dropped to his knee so quickly, she heard it bump against the wooden floor in the middle of the café. A couple of women in their mid-twenties who were lunching turned towards them and giggled. She had just told him her parents were leaving within a month and told her they would be selling the house to buy another in Perth, and as such, she couldn't go to the beach with him after her shift, as she needed to begin her search for a room to rent.

'Marry me,' he said, grabbing her hand.

'Stop it, get off the floor,' she said sternly, pulling her hand away.

'Not until you say yes.'

'I didn't tell you about my parents so you could ask me to marry you,' she said.

'I was going to ask anyway. This is perfect timing.'

'In the middle of my workplace? How romantic.' She feigned a swoon.

His face grew sombre, and he slowly rose from the floor. 'I'm sorry,' he said.

'I'm kidding, silly,' she replied, seeing he had taken her seriously. 'You could ask me in a soup kitchen, anywhere, and I would say yes.'

'Does that mean …?'

Mary realised what she had just said. Sure it was too soon, only having dated him for a couple of months, but now when she envisioned her life, she couldn't fathom one without Gary in it. 'If that's what you really want.' She saw his eyes widen in excitement. 'Then yes, I will marry you.'

Her heart ached and yet she held on to that moment, where her life stretched beyond her, where everything was going to be wonderful, where she would live out her days with the man she loved, the man who adored her. She pushed past the thoughts of his moods, the loneliness she felt sometimes when he was even in the same room as her, when he crawled into the depths of his mind, a place he didn't allow her to go with him. She still tried to feel like the twenty-year-old whose heart was so full of hope as she stared at the man who bruised his knee asking for her hand in marriage.

Mary wandered to the shore and let the water lap around her ankles. The cold of the sea in the soft moonlit night soothed her mind and she looked to the moon, hidden by thick grey clouds. She hoped Gary was there, watching over her, over them. Soon Lucille would be gone to university in Melbourne, and Marina would be more alone than ever. And after Marina left, who knew what? She turned back and walked into the quiet house, turning out the light.

CHAPTER 14

'Can I stay at the house for a little while?' Virginia was seated on the stool while Mary made her a cup of tea. She had popped in without the girls and Mary was a little surprised she didn't have them with her. She never came by on her own, so Mary left her wet washing in the basket and offered her something to drink, which Virginia gratefully accepted. Mary was shocked at this question though.

'Erm ...' she stammered.

'Just for about a week, maybe two?'

'I think that should be okay,' said Mary, quickly calculating the space left in the boarding house. There was her room, the girls' room, the Davises' room and an older gentleman passing through town, who would be here for the next night, took another. She was in the process of cleaning out the room just vacated by a regular, a one-night stopover, and the only other room left would be the one she left empty just in case Lawrence came through unexpectedly. 'What about the girls?'

'They won't be staying. They are with their father's parents, up in Wollongong.' She sniffed in irritation. 'Do you have a full house? The carpark wasn't full.'

Just like Virginia to notice, thought Mary. But she realised she was being unkind. Virginia needed a place to stay and she could make room. Right then the bell on the door sounded and Mary excused herself. She always felt a thump in her chest at the sound and was always disappointed when it was a delivery person or a guest who wasn't Lawrence.

Her heart dropped as it always did. A young couple stood at the desk and Mary set about giving them Lawrence's room. Virginia would have to wait until she had cleaned the other room out. She settled them in and went back to the kitchen where Virginia was already drinking the tea she had made for herself.

'Hope you don't mind,' she said.

'Not at all. Glad for the help. Besides, you know your way around here quite well.'

After she had set up the room for Virginia, Mary collected the slips for dinner. Only the Davises and Virginia wanted a meal, which was unusual for such a crowded house, but Mary was glad for it. It had been a busy day and she kept reminding herself to change the description of the boarding house to 'Bed and Breakfast'. Without staff, it was getting too tiring; she realised she wasn't as young as she used to be, her energy running out much more quickly these days.

After dinner was served and she and the girls had eaten Mary had tried to help Marina with her homework, but her daughter had resisted.

'Leave her alone,' mouthed Lucille from the other end of the dining table and Mary had nodded. The Davises were out for a walk, which was unusual for them on a night as cool as this one.

She went out to the porch as she usually did in the

evening and sat on the armchair, putting her feet up on the footstool. They were stinging and she wanted to go to the water to give them a soak, but her body was tired. Just as she lay her head back and closed her eyes, she heard the creak of the screen door and squeezed her eyes in exasperation.

'May I join you?' Virginia said softly.

'Sure,' said Mary, opening her eyes and putting her feet back on the ground.

Virginia took a seat on one of the porch chairs and stared ahead into the dark evening. There was an awkward silence for a few minutes, Mary not knowing what to say and too tired to think about it. Virginia had a glass of wine in her hand, which she sipped at nervously.

The silhouette of the Davises came into view and Mary turned to watch them walking together, hand in hand, slowly, surely. Virginia turned her head to the sight of them too.

'I wanted that,' said Virginia, her voice soft, a little shaky.

'Hmm,' replied Mary, knowingly.

'It's too late for me now.'

Mary had the feeling that Virginia wanted some encouragement to continue, but she didn't want to know. She was too tired to focus on anything but again she thought she was being unkind to this woman who was obviously in pain sitting by her side and begging to be heard. 'Is it really too late?' she asked, turning to Virginia.

'I think so. I don't think he's going to leave that trollop.' She said it without emotion.

'What makes you say that?' Mary cringed at her question; it sounded so intrusive. 'Maybe it's … I don't know, a phase, like you said before?'

'I thought so too at first, but Chester, he insists it's over between us.' Mary didn't know what to say to this so she stayed quiet. 'He doesn't touch me anymore, not like he used to when we were first together. He hasn't touched me in, I don't know, more than a year.' Still there wasn't any expression in her voice. 'This is my last-ditch attempt to get him back. I'm hoping he misses me and comes to find me.' She looked at Mary, her eyes narrowed. 'No one knows I'm here, just Chester.' It seemed like a weird little warning for Mary not to spread the news about town.

Mary swallowed to keep her words at bay. Of course that was why she was here. That's why she brought her girls here. No one in their right mind would suspect that Virginia, the queen bee, was holing up at Mary's place. In this town though, how long would that remain a secret? 'Sure,' said Mary and put her feet back on the footstool. She tried to find some compassion for this woman and even felt pity for her, but she was the same old selfish Virginia, without a thought for anyone else's feelings.

Virginia took a deep breath and raised her nearly empty glass. She smiled widely, a forced smile. 'Onward and upward, hey?' She downed the remainder of her wine. 'But after this, I'm not waiting around for him anymore. It's time to move on.' She got off the chair and headed to the door. She opened it and looked back. 'You have any single men friends?'

Mary chuckled and shook her head.

'Well, if you see any come through here, you be sure to let me know.' She turned to go and turned around again. 'Good ones, not louts.' She cocked her head. 'Well, I guess they wouldn't be staying here if they had money.' She shrugged and shut the door and left Mary with her teeth clenched tight.

'Some things don't change,' Mary muttered to herself as the Davises mounted the stairs.

CHAPTER 15

It had been a week since Virginia had moved in and she'd made her presence felt. The Davises had had enough and left the room every time Virginia entered it and even though Virginia followed Mary around like a lost puppy and Mary tolerated her, she didn't give her much of a chance to get under her skin, the same thick skin she had tried to acquire from her teenage years because of Virginia. Virginia didn't attempt to chat with the girls, who were happy to stay away from the woman who seemed to put them down all the time.

'Why are you wearing your hair like that?' she called to Lucille, who turned to her, fluffed her hair out with her hands and smiled back without a word.

'What is with those pants? They look like something my mother wore when she was a child,' she said once to Marina, who just scowled and left the room.

'Just stay out of her way,' said Mary when she went to check in on them when they were getting ready for bed.

'Why is she here?' asked Lucille.

'She just needs a place to stay for a while. She'll be gone soon.'

'She's horrible,' said Marina making a face.

'She has problems. She is not horrible, just complicated.'

'Why are you making excuses for her?'

'Because some people need excuses to explain who they are,' said Mary, wishing she didn't have to try to explain who Virginia was. For all her own experience, there was nothing that Virginia did to endear herself to Mary. But she couldn't throw her out, not for making thoughtless comments and being selfish. She knew what Virginia was when she took her in. 'Just one more week. Please, just bear with her for another seven days?'

Marina made a grunt and turned around in her bed and Lucille rolled her eyes. Mary kissed them both and left the room.

It was in the second week when everything went crazy. Sophie came to stay unexpectedly and two of the other guests had booked in for a week each, highly unusual for winter. Mary put Sophie in what she silently referred to as Lawrence's room and was relieved that she had changed the advertisement in the local paper and on the storefront to 'Bed and Breakfast' the day after Virginia had arrived. It had been a relief not to prepare meals for all the guests, but she did cook for the Davises who she considered part of the family. Virginia insisted she had come before the change occurred and Mary was happy to make an extra meal for her too.

'House full!' Sophie walked with Mary to the edge of the water. 'I hope I didn't put you out.'

'Mary put her arm around Sophie. 'I would let you sleep in my room if there wasn't space. You are welcome anytime.'

'How long has it been since I've been coming here?'

'Gosh, I don't know!' Mary tried to think. 'Maybe five, six years?'

'Wow, that long since I've been a has-been.'

'Stop it. You're not a has-been.'

'Yeah,' sulked Sophie. 'More like a never-was.'

'More like the most famous person I know.'

'That doesn't say much,' Sophie replied. 'No offence. By the way, how long is that one going to be staying?' She shook her head towards the porch where Virginia was sunning herself.

Mary nudged her friend and frowned at her. But she could already see Sophie, like everyone else, was irritated by the constant presence and chatter of Virginia. 'Maybe a week more, maybe two. Who knows?'

'What's her story?'

Mary shrugged. She didn't want to be the bearer of gossip, but she had to give Sophie some sort of answer. Besides, Virginia didn't seem to care about her secret anymore, she told everyone who was around about her troubles, about her lost love, about the mistake Chester was making in leaving her. 'She's having some issues at home. She just needed to get away.'

'Hmph. I'd say he's the one that got away, from her! Smart man, but now you're stuck with her.'

'She's all right ...'

'You're too nice. Just know that I'm not going to be as nice as you,' said Sophie. 'Anyway, enough about her; tell me about Lawrence. Has he been coming around?'

'No, not since that time ...'

'The time you nearly smooched,' laughed Sophie, kissing

the air.

'Stop it! There was no smooching.'

'My darling lady, you are too pure.' She took Mary's hand and held on to it. 'I must teach you some of my wily ways.' She raised her eyebrows cheekily and Mary laughed.

'I'm just fine. I have the girls, the boarding house ...'

'But you don't have a man.'

'It's the seventies, Sophie. I don't need a man.'

'Maybe not,' said Sophie thoughtfully. 'But then again, you already have a man—the ghost of your husband who lives by your side.' Mary narrowed her eyes and Sophie grinned apologetically. 'I'm sorry, I know you miss him, but you have to move on.'

'I told you ...'

'I know, I know, the girls, the boarding house. But by the time the girls have flown the coop, you will not ... you know.'

'You mean I won't be attractive to prospective husbands?' Mary laughed and tossed her braid over her shoulder. 'I think that ship has sailed.'

'You must stop fishing for compliments,' said Sophie. 'You are an attractive woman and I sometimes worry about you alone in the house.'

'Again, I'm not alone.'

'Are you talking about those little old folks who live with you? They are lovely, yes, but if anything were to happen, I somehow don't see them overpowering a potential rapist.'

'Oh Sophie, don't talk like that!' Mary exclaimed, but it wasn't anything she hadn't thought of herself; she always had a steak knife safely tucked under the reception desk.

They had turned back and Mary looked at the house, a cosy glowing beacon on the sandy hill. It wasn't just a job, something that kept her afloat. To her it was where she had dreamed of the future with Gary, had raised her children, and even though she kept it running to make money, she realised it was something she really enjoyed. And this last week had been much better, not having to run around trying to buy ingredients for the advertised meal. Her future was looking brighter and it didn't take a man to make it so. She loved this place. It was her home.

CHAPTER 16

It was a Saturday and Mary had been out shopping with Lucille for a dress for her formal. Mary was a little stung that Lucille wanted to buy a dress rather than have her mother make one for her, especially since at this time of year, every year, she received so many orders from the local high school students for them. But she also understood that Lucille wanted something new and something she could shop for. It was rare they went shopping for outfits together and Mary was pleased that Lucille still wanted her mother's company and opinion. Marina had wanted to stay home as usual to do her homework and understanding her daughter's need for privacy and some alone time, Mary conceded.

It had been a long day with Lucille wanting to go into every shop in the city of Melbourne, more than four hours away from Righteous Creek. She had finally chosen a dress, one of the first she'd seen, a long backless emerald gown, which Mary had sniffed at for its lack of coverage. But it could have been worse; they had seen so many outfits that left very little to the imagination.

It was close to six p.m. when she arrived home and turning her car through the wooden gates of the parking area, she saw his blue Ford Falcon.

'Hey, Lawrence is here!' exclaimed Lucille.

95

'Yes, I see,' replied Mary, her throat suddenly feeling very dry.

'I thought he wouldn't come back,' she said, her hand already reaching for the door handle before Mary had driven into her parking space.

'Now, Lucille!' She pulled up the brake and put her hand on her daughter's arm. 'Don't go throwing yourself at him. You're much too mature for that now.'

'I never!' Lucille looked at her mother indignantly and crossed her arms.

'I'm not trying to embarrass you, but you are nearly a grown woman.' Mary wasn't sure if she was warning her daughter because she was afraid Lawrence would be taken by her advances or because she didn't want Lucille to make a fool of herself. All she knew was that she wanted more time in the car to compose herself, to cool her heating cheeks before she came face to face with him. She could already feel her heart rate quicken and was irritated about the way she felt. It had been more than six months since she'd seen him and for the most part, she had managed to keep him out of her mind.

Lucille rolled her eyes. Then she grinned. 'I was a bit silly last year, wasn't I?' She sighed and slumped in her seat. 'But he was so dreamy, Mum.'

Mary cleared her throat and resisted a giggle. Lucille always spoke her mind and nothing embarrassed her anymore. She knew who she was, who she wanted to be. She knew Lawrence was off limits.

She looked at Mary through narrowed eyes. 'What about you, Mum?'

Mary was taken aback. 'What about me?' She knew what her daughter was asking but needed a second to work out how to respond.

'You and Lawrence. I saw you guys dance that night. You seemed, I don't know … good.'

'He is a young man, Lu,' said Mary, taking her keys out of the ignition. This was not a conversation to be had with her daughter.

'You're young too,' insisted Lucille.

'Stop it. C'mon, let's show your dress to Marina.'

As Lucille got out of the car and collected her things from the boot, Mary glanced into the rear-view mirror, quickly assessing her reflection. She sighed. There wasn't much to do about the bags that hung under her eyes. It had been an early start to a very long day.

She turned the corner of the house to find Lawrence sitting on the porch with Marina, the pen in her hand furiously scribbling across the page, his head bent towards her, holding her textbook. Mary paused for a moment and smiled at the sight of them.

'Larry!' Lucille bounded past her, carting her shopping bags.

'Lucille!' Mary scolded. Never once had the man asked to be called anything but his full name and here was her daughter becoming familiar with him.

Lucille ignored her and ran to Lawrence, deposited her bags on the floor beside him, and threw herself into his arms. Lawrence, for his part, accepted her hug with a broad smile and a 'Hi, Lu!'

Mary hovered on the bottom step and waited for
Lawrence to extricate himself from Lucille, but looking over her
shoulder, he gave Mary a warm smile, his eyes not leaving hers.
Mary blinked and turned to Marina, who was gaping at Lucille,
something like annoyance in her eyes.

'Hello, Mary,' said Lawrence.

Lucille had gathered her bags off the floor. 'Come on,
Marina, let me show you what I got. Maybe when it's your time,
you can use it too. It's too beautiful to use just once.' Marina
reluctantly rose and followed her sister into the house. 'It's green,
but not a vile green, you know like the ties Mr Jones wears ...'
Her voice trailed off into the house, leaving Mary staring after
them.

She turned to Lawrence, who had his eyes fixed on her.
She shifted to one foot, leaning on the banister, and Lawrence
came forward, standing on the step above hers.

'Hello, Mary,' he repeated.

'Hello, Lawrence,' she croaked and pushed her hair
behind her ears.

'How are you?'

'Good. I had to take Lucille to the city. She needed a
dress for her formal. I was going to sew one for her, but she
preferred to buy one this time, probably an excuse to go into
Melbourne.' She knew she was babbling but she couldn't stop.
'It's only a couple of weeks away and I thought it was best we got
it out of the way. She was excited too. But it was a long drive and
Melbourne is so busy now. I don't know how people live there.
Have you been there lately?' She paused as Lawrence curled his

lip in amusement. This just made her angry. She wanted to ask him where he had been all this time. Why he hadn't called. Had he found better lodgings? Had he found a woman? 'How are you?' she enquired instead.

'I've been well. Just busy.'

'You haven't been back,' she couldn't resist saying.

'No.' He lowered his head. 'No,' he said again, and then, facing her again, reached out his hand to move the stray hair that kept fluttering against her face. The touch of his hand was like a hot rod, but she let it burn against her cheek for a second before he removed it.

'Found someplace better?' She gave a little laugh, trying to lighten the mood which was taking too intense a turn.

'No.' It was the third no from him.

She suddenly remembered there was no room in the boarding house. 'Oh, Lawrence,' she exclaimed.

'No room at the inn?'

She looked at him in dismay. She had a full house, his room now occupied by Sophie. She shook her head. 'No,' she whispered softly.

'I know. Your friend in there told me.' He chuckled. 'She offered to let me share her room. But I haven't removed my luggage from my car anyway. I can stay elsewhere.'

Bloody Virginia, thought Mary. *If she hadn't parked herself here for who knows how long, there would be room for him.* 'Are you here for long?' She was trying to think, while hoping that he was planning an extended trip. She could do what they did last time. The girls would be fine with sharing with her for a while and the last time, Lucille had spent more time in Mary's bed, her chin rested on her shoulder, reading *The Godfather* until she fell asleep. She was sure they wouldn't mind, especially since it was Lawrence who they would be sacrificing their room for.

'I was hoping to spend a couple of weeks. I should have called first.'

'No, I just never …' She made up her mind. 'Stay. We can manage.'

'Where will you put me?' He sounded incredulous, but a teasing smile curled his lip.

'We've done this before, remember?' She shrugged.

'But …'

'No buts,' she said. 'Follow me.'

'I need to get my things from the car.'

'Well, not before you help me set up the room first,' she laughed. He followed her to the door and she opened it. Then she turned around to find his face a few inches from hers. 'By the way, if you knew the house was full, why did you wait?' she said more boldly than she felt.

His eyes stared intently at her and she swallowed, her hand gripping the handle of the door. 'I wanted to see you.'

She swallowed hard again, spun on her heel and went inside.

CHAPTER 17

It was working, at least for the first few days. Marina spent most of her time holed up in their room but Lucille preferred to do her studies at the kitchen table when Mary made dinner. The weather had turned pleasant almost overnight, leaving room in the back garden, that was filled with little flowering plants, for anyone who wanted to spend some time outdoors. Of course, the sea in spring was a glorious sight, and most of the visitors took out their folding chairs and dotted themselves around the perimeter of the house, even the Davises, who were loath to stray too far from the house, save for the occasional walk.

Although the girls were bunked in with Mary at night and their clothes were squeezed tightly into the wardrobe with hers, it didn't seem too much of an inconvenience and the only time Mary felt it was when she needed a minute on her own, to quell the flush that covered her face when Lawrence looked at her in that particular way, or when she found herself imagining brazen thoughts of him.

It became a routine for them all. Lawrence waking before anyone else, making himself a cup of coffee and sitting out on the porch. Mary would arise at six thirty and drink her coffee while she prepared the breakfast.

'Need help?' Lawrence would come in and not heeding

her pleas that she could manage, set about bringing out the cutlery and crockery, placing them in a neat row on the kitchen table. This left them time to have a cup of coffee together while they waited for the rest of the house to rise. The others would come in around eight and seat themselves around the two tables in the hall, Marina and Lucille sitting at the table in the kitchen. Virginia, now considering herself part of the family, placed herself in the kitchen as well, to the chagrin of Sophie, who would waltz in at nine, take a look at the jabbering Virginia, make a face and ask for her breakfast to be brought into the hall. She would then place herself next to the Davises, who were fond of the woman with her tales of movie sets and dashing co-stars.

Virginia always tried to seat herself next to Lawrence, and the irritation was evident on her face when that spot was taken. It didn't stop her from leaning over someone else to flutter her eyelids at the man who didn't seem to have any reaction to her, distasteful or otherwise. Virginia had been different since Lawrence arrived. She at first eyed him subtly and when it didn't seem as if he were falling under her spell, she became more bold, searching him out, and wherever Lawrence was, Virginia was not far behind.

'She's got a thing for him,' muttered Sophie, who was helping Mary finish washing the dishes.

Mary chuckled. 'Yes, I've noticed.'

'Well? How do you feel about that?' Sophie demanded.

Mary wiped her hands on the dishcloth and leaned against the sink. She had thought about it, the first day Lawrence arrived. Of course she didn't want Virginia to get anywhere near Lawrence, but she also thought it may be a way out of her burgeoning feelings for him. If Virginia could 'steal' him away, then he wasn't worth having anyway. Sure, she may be a little cut up about it, but it would also take some pressure off her. Then she may look at him in a different light. As it was, she felt she and Lawrence were trying to dismiss their feelings, talking of inconsequential things, such as the weather, the girls' schoolwork, nothing that really mattered, like where he had been for all that time. Where did he go? Did he have a lover? A wife even! But all these questions would be moot if Virginia conveniently stepped in. Unfortunately, he didn't seem to give Virginia a second look, answering her questions with monosyllabic answers.

'Well?'

'Whatever happens, happens,' Mary said dully. With the house, her sewing and the girls keeping her busy, she didn't have time for romances that would upset the routine of her life, especially those that were bound to go nowhere.

'He looks at you all the time, you know,' whispered Sophie.

Mary flushed. 'You're imagining things, seeing what you want to see.'

'Well, I notice things. He doesn't take a second look at me when you're in the room, and even when you're not in the room. His eyes follow you around everywhere.'

Mary's chest warmed at the thought. 'I wouldn't know,' she replied.

Sophie gave an exaggerated sigh. 'Okay, I'll take that for now.' She whispered, narrowing her eyes towards the door, 'But only because that bat-faced woman is coming down the hallway.' She hung the dishcloth over the sink. 'You really ought to get a dishwasher. Nearly everyone has them now.'

Mary laughed. 'Can't afford it,' she replied. 'Besides. I enjoy this. It's relaxing and the only time I have to think.'

'Well, think about him,' said Sophie in her ear and ducked out of the path of the dishcloth that was flying her way.

'Morning, Virginia,' said Mary, as Virginia sauntered through the kitchen door. 'Still hungry?'

'No,' said Virginia and placed herself at the table, fingering the salt and pepper shakers.

'A cup of tea? Coffee?'

'No, thanks,' said Virginia, and Mary turned on the tap, scrubbing at the teaspoon she still had in her hand. She could see the woman wanted to say something and she wasn't sure if she had the gumption for it today. She had had a busy morning, coaxing Marina out of bed. Lucille had lost her maths book and was running about frantically and when Mary tried to help her find it, Marina promptly hopped back into bed. Then Lucille was out the door, running to catch her bus, not waiting for Marina. She had a big test that morning and was in a minor panic.

'Excuse me, Virginia,' said Mary and ran back to their room to try to coax Marina out of bed again, amongst many protestations, and it was only when she heard Lawrence's voice in the hallway that she jumped out of bed. By then the bus had come and gone and it would be another hour before the next one came by. Marina would be late if she walked the thirty-five minutes it took to get to school.

Once Marina had begun to dress, Mary stepped out and leaned against the door. It was getting frustrating, but she had heard teenagers were like this. Lucille hadn't been so annoying, so she thought she got lucky. She sighed and rested her head on the door. Still two years before Marina was an adult and school was finished. They were certainly going to drag.

'Need some help?' Lawrence came into the hallway and leaned against the wall. He looked so cool, so unbothered, Mary envied him. But what did she really know of his life? People had problems no one knew about, and Lawrence, for all she knew, could have another full life with another family somewhere else and used her boarding house as a place to get away from it.

'No, she's fine. Just going to be late, that's all. Third time this week. I'm probably going to get a note from the school.'

'I can drive her there,' offered Lawrence.

'No, of course not,' said Mary. She had been doing that far too often herself, hurrying with the breakfast and leaving the dishes for when she returned. She hated to do that, have a messy kitchen and dining hall, especially when she had other work that needed doing. If Sophie was around, she helped, but she couldn't count on Sophie doing that all the time. She may be a good friend, but she was also a guest.

'I insist,' said Lawrence. Then his eyes widened. 'Oh sorry, I'm overstepping again.'

'No, you're not.' Mary realised that Lawrence thought she didn't trust him. 'I just don't want to put you out.' Of course she trusted Lawrence; as little as she knew about him, she knew he cared about her and her daughters.

'Well, I'm heading out to the post office anyway, so it's no problem.'

Mary conceded. 'Okay, only if it's not a bother.'

Lawrence peered at her as if about to say something. Then he nodded. 'I'll be waiting on the porch.'

Where else would he be? thought Mary. He loved the porch, spent most of his time there, on the far right side, ever so close to her bedroom window. She heard him cough sometimes, quite late into the night, and she'd often wondered what he did out there, alone in the dark, by himself. What could he be thinking about?

'Tap's still running,' called Virginia, bringing Mary running back into the kitchen. Virginia was still sitting at the table, sipping on her tea, seemingly oblivious to the water that ran straight into the drain. Mary shook her head as she turned off the tap. Virginia behaved worse than a child sometimes.

She turned to Virginia, who was biting on the corner of her lower lip, her nails tapping slowly on the table. Mary took a deep breath and began to clear the table, which she wished she could leave for later. Right now she just wanted a minute to herself before she changed the bed linen and headed off to do her chores but Virginia clearly had something on her mind that she wanted to share with Mary.

'Lawrence went out,' said Virginia. It wasn't a question.

'Yes,' said Mary, trying not to encourage a fuller conversation.

'When will he be back?'

'I don't know. He had some things to do.' Mary didn't want to talk to Virginia about Lawrence.

'Can we have a talk?'

Mary took a deep breath. 'Sure,' she said and wiped her hands on her apron. She was about to sit down, but Virginia began to rise.

'Do you have time to take a little walk?'

Mary took off her apron and wished she was harder, that she could just refuse, but Virginia had something on her mind that was troubling her. She followed Virginia out of the house. She didn't have much time today. She had to do the shopping at Geelong; she was running out of things to cook for breakfast. For some reason lately, instead of their usual cereal, the Davises were indulging in bacon and eggs, and the young couple, Natalie and Russell, had wanted pancakes for the week they had been here. Since that was on the menu, she couldn't very well tell them she had run out. She had some stocking up to do. Besides that, she had to do the turndowns of the rooms and provide fresh towels and sheets. She would have to put off the washing until tomorrow.

She took a deep breath of the fresh sea air and pulled her cardigan around her. The breeze was cool. She wondered what Virginia wanted and they had reached the water's edge before Virginia began.

'How old is Lawrence?' she asked.

'I'm not entirely sure,' replied Mary, taken aback by the question and unwilling to divulge any information like that to her.

'Do you think he's a little young for me?'

Mary blanched.

'It's just, I think he might like me.' She waited for a response, but Mary was too shocked to reply. She knew Virginia had been trying to flirt with Lawrence, but she never for a moment thought she could be so blunt. 'He's very handsome, and broody. Do you know his story?'

Mary cleared her throat. 'No, I don't. He's a guest here and I don't make enquiries as to their lives.' She felt a shiver of jealousy which caught her by surprise. She'd been aware of Virginia's little crush but now that Virginia had voiced it, the green-eyed monster tore at her heart.

'But what do you know about him?' Virginia insisted.

'It's none of our business,' snapped Mary and was even more surprised at herself. It came out much harsher than she'd meant it to and Virginia recoiled. 'I'm sorry, I just don't think we should pry, you know?'

Virginia gave her a strange look. 'Do you ...' She left her sentence hanging and Mary felt herself redden.

There was an awkward silence, unfamiliar to Mary when Virginia was around. 'Here he is now,' said Mary as she spotted Lawrence's car pull into the carpark. She was grateful for the interruption to their conversation that was taking a rather awkward turn and the two women walked back to the house in silence.

What do I know about him? Mary asked herself as she drove to Geelong. She was sure Virginia was going to ask to come with her and was relieved when she didn't but she suddenly realised she was back at the house with him. She felt her chest tighten at the thought of them together and she suddenly knew she wouldn't be okay if something happened between them. She hadn't felt that way about Gary; with Gary, she was secure in his love, from the moment she met him. But with Lawrence, she didn't know how to feel. He was not hers. She wasn't even sure if he was someone else's. What she did know was how she felt when she was around him and it was something she was beginning to enjoy, her guilt about Gary lessening with each interaction with Lawrence.

She turned into the parking lot of the supermarket and turned off the ignition. This situation needed to come to a head, whatever that was going to be. But his age, she thought, and blushed. He's so young, what if we aren't compatible in … Her face was now hot and she opened the car door, shaking her head at the audacity of her thoughts.

CHAPTER 18

'When is she leaving?' whispered Mrs Davis one morning when Virginia slunk into the kitchen, still in her nightgown, a silky number which flowed over her curves with abandon.

Mary had noticed a change in Virginia after her chat with her a few days earlier. Before, she spent a lot of time on the house phone, calling her friends, complaining loudly about her husband and pretending to be somewhere else, or she would wander around throwing herself into conversations, and Mary had felt sorry for her, understanding her loneliness. She complained about missing her children but made no move to contact them and Mary wondered how they were getting along without their mother.

Now there was a subtle difference; she was quieter than usual, but still slunk around, her eyes darting between Mary and Lawrence when they were in the same room together. She sat around the lounge and when she wasn't, she lay out on the beach chair with not much more on than a bikini and a hat, even on days when the sun wasn't out.

Mary shrugged. She was quite over Virginia staying here, but she didn't have the heart to ask her when she was leaving.

'It's a full house,' said Mrs Davis loudly.

'Hush, Mrs Davis,' said Mary, hoping the woman's idea of hinting didn't offend any of the other guests who may be wandering around. 'Anyway, I think Natalie and Russell are leaving the day after tomorrow.'

'They aren't the ones I'm talking about,' sulked Mrs Davis, giving Virginia a glare as she walked out of the room.

Virginia pretended not to hear the conversation and sat at the kitchen table, a habit Mary was still not used to and still not fond of. Mary sighed. She would have to figure it out. Virginia was isolating most of the guests and it wasn't good for business. Besides, she had overstayed by more than a week which she hadn't paid for. Mary had turned down three other guests, paying customers who had called in looking for a room.

It was in the early evening when Natalie suggested a bonfire. It was to celebrate her last evening at the house, and as it was a Friday, Mary obliged. There was too much tension in the house and they all needed something to lighten the mood. For the first time in a while, Virginia perked up and drove out to the store to buy alcohol. Mary was a bit relieved. It may make Virginia loose enough to ask her what her plans were.

****

It was a beautiful evening, almost perfect, the sky filled with stars, a gentle breeze that flowed through the spring evening bringing with it the taste of salt and the smell of hope. The music had been playing loudly, the guests were happy, there was dancing and even Marina came out for a little while, sitting by Lawrence, who couldn't keep his eyes off Mary. Sophie sat by Mary when she was tired from shimmying, and kept nudging her to ask Lawrence to dance, so much so that Mary got up and walked about, smiling and encouraging the guests to take to the dance floor and offering refreshments. She was enjoying this evening. There was a sense of freedom and of happiness and it permeated the air.

She kept her eye on Marina who sat close to Lawrence who chatted easily with her and she felt a twinge of envy that her daughter could be so relaxed in the presence of someone whom she barely knew and yet couldn't even confide in her own mother. She didn't know what to do about it anymore. She had tried talking to her, leaving her alone, even nagging her, and nothing was working, so she was trying patience right now, hoping that it was in fact just the stage that Lucille had suggested it were.

Marina got up and went into the house and Mary frowned, watching the front door to see whether she would return. It was still early and Mary prayed she would. It wasn't often she saw her daughter with such a satisfied smile on her face. When she saw Marina return with a glass of Coke in her hand, she was relieved, but when she saw Marina's eyes narrow as she looked towards Lawrence, she turned to follow her gaze. Virginia had taken Marina's seat and was leaning into Lawrence. She turned back to her daughter who was already retreating back into the house.

Mary pursed her lips. Virginia was really getting on everyone's nerves and was now interfering in the wellbeing of her child. She would deal with her tomorrow, she made up her mind; something had to be done. She followed Marina into the house and after calling for her with no response, she checked her bedroom where Marina had already donned her nightdress and was in the process of getting into bed.

'Come out, Marina,' coaxed Mary. 'The night is still young. It's beautiful out.'

'I'm fine,' said Marina, her eyes on the wall behind Mary, her brows straight and unflinching, even as Mary sat on the bed.

'But it's still early. You don't have to get up early tomorrow.'

'I'm fine,' Marina said and pursed her lips in irritation.

She tried a different tack. 'Natalie and Russell are really shaking it up. I think with one more drink, it will be worth staying up for,' she said, tickling Marina's feet.

Marina moved her feet away. 'I'm fine,' she repeated and pulled the blanket over her head.

Mary lowered her head in disappointment. She knew she wasn't going to get her daughter back outside tonight. Marina was more stubborn than ever and after Mary pulled the blanket from Marina's face, kissed the warm cheek and tucked the blanket around her shoulders, she walked to the door. She glanced back at her child, feeling helpless, the pit in her stomach at Marina's temperament lately feeling heavier than ever. She had no idea how to help her child. She didn't know what the problem was, and Marina didn't talk to her as she used to. She turned off the light, leaving Marina's face shining in the moonlight that crept through the window, still unmoved, the glint of a tear rolling slowly down her face.

She returned outside and saw Lawrence at the bonfire,

stoking the wood. His face was bent forward, a slight frown highlighted by the glow of the flames. She leaned on the banister and observed the party and couldn't help but smile. Sophie was laughing with the Davises who had come out tonight to bid farewell to Natalie and Russell, Poopy their dog scampering around trying to sniff out bits of fallen food. Their shared dislike for Virginia had made them close in the two weeks since the couple had been here. She smiled at Moira, the waif, who had also been there for nearly two weeks, and also without a plan to move on.

Mary cocked her head at Moira, pale, with big brown eyes, almost black, that looked fearful all the time. Although she had never told her age, Mary guessed she wasn't much older than Lucille. She came in one early morning, nothing with her but a backpack which looked empty, and Mary knew immediately that she was in need of help as she walked up the front steps of Jesse's Boarding. Mary had put down her cup of coffee which she had first sipped a second earlier.

'Hello,' she had said hopping from one foot to another. 'Do you have room for one?'

Mary pretended not to see the fresh bruise on her forehead, or the droplets of blood that sat dry on her white blouse. 'Yes, of course we do,' said Mary, knowing well that this was not going to be a guest who paid up front. But there was a spare room and she was not going to let this little urchin go back to from wherever she came.

Moira still hadn't opened up about her situation and Mary was not going to prod her about it. She was no trouble, apart from the fact that she hadn't paid for her room, but Mary had found work for her at the café in town and Moira was an eager employee, promising to pay Mary the next week when her first pay cheque came in. She usually kept to herself, staying in her room, except for when she came out at breakfast, and taking night walks alone. Mary worried about her and her situation but tonight she had a big smile on her face as she watched Russell and Natalie jive on the sand.

Lucille was standing a little further away from the group, a soft drink in her hand and a young man by her side. Mary had seen this boy before, a respectful senior at the school, who she knew had been trying to find the right time to ask if he could take Lucille to the formal. Virginia was nowhere to be seen and Mary craned her neck to see if she could be seen along the water. She wasn't there. Mary shrugged, somewhat relieved that Virginia was not around. She was just irritating everyone and the amount of alcohol she'd consumed had certainly not endeared her to anyone.

Mary glanced at her watch, which showed just after seven thirty p.m. She looked back towards the house, wondering if she should go back in to try to cajole Marina out, and thought better of it. She strolled over to where Sophie sat and rested her hand on the back of her chair. Sophie patted her arm and smiled up at her. She then raised her eyebrows in the direction of Lawrence and pulled at Mary's arm. Mary rolled her eyes and bent forward, knowing what was coming.

'Just so you know, Virginia and him,' she whispered, nodding towards Lawrence. 'They had some sort of argument. Then she stormed off.'

Mary was taken aback. What sort of argument could Lawrence and Virginia have had? They barely knew each other. Maybe there was more to them than she thought. She looked towards Lawrence, the frown still on his face but heading back to his seat. He leaned back and took a swig from his bottle of beer. His eyes landed on Mary's, and she felt a sudden absence of fear. She walked slowly over to him and took the vacant seat beside him.

'How's Marina?' he asked.

'She's … I don't know,' she replied honestly. 'You probably know more than I do. She barely talks to me anymore.'

'She will be okay. There's a lot going on with her … She's a teenager.' He had a wistful look in his eyes.

'I hope she grows out of it.' She looked towards the water again. 'Where's Virginia?'

'I don't know,' he said, leaning forward in his chair.

'Did you upset her?'

'It wouldn't take much to upset Virginia,' he replied with a grin.

'Okay, what did you say to her?'

He let out a little chuckle and then looked remorseful. 'I … um … didn't take her up on her offer.'

Mary could feel her ears begin to heat. She swallowed. 'And what offer was that?'

'To … er … you know.' Even through the colours of the fire bouncing off his face, she could see him blush.

Mary tried to suppress a smile, putting her fisted hands over her mouth. It didn't fool him.

'Don't make fun,' he said, frowning.

'I'm not making fun,' she replied, but her mind was spinning. She couldn't believe he had refused Virginia. Well, not that she couldn't believe it, she was just overjoyed that he had.

'Can I ask why you didn't take her up on it?'

'She's not my type,' he said. Then he turned to her, his eyes piercing through hers, and it was her turn to blush. 'Besides, I'm in love with someone else.'

'Oh?'

He nodded and looked at the fire again. Mary wasn't sure now if he meant her, or someone else altogether. She wasn't sure she hoped it was the former. She changed the subject. It was getting to be too much for her. 'Tell me about your life, Lawrence.'

He looked back at her, surprise in his eyes. 'There's not much to tell.'

'Everyone has a story,' she said and looked up at the stars, so brightly twinkling, she was filled with a new hope.

'What about you?'

'I have a story. A sad one, a happy one. But what you see is what you get. I'm no great mystery. I live to make my girls happy. I live to provide for them, and that's where I get my happiness.'

'And the sadness you talk of?'

'You know that too. My husband. So long ago, but the hurt is still there.'

He took her hand and Mary didn't even think to consider they were surrounded by people. She let her fingers clutch at hope, at a feeling she hadn't felt in so long. The touch of a man. The touch of Lawrence. His eyes bore through hers and it was as if there were nothing in the world but the two of them.

She heard the call the third time.

'Mum!'

The spell was broken and she quickly grabbed her hand back, turning around to see her daughter looking down at her in astonishment.

'What, what is it, Lu?' She jumped to her feet, her throat drying.

Lucille had a strange little smile on her lips, a grin of satisfaction. 'Just wanted to let you know I'm going for a walk on the beach with Kyle.' Mary leaned forward to look at Kyle, who was nervously kicking the sand with his toe. He looked up and Mary smiled at him. He smiled back, a little more confidently. 'Okay, but not too far and not too late.'

'Thanks, Mum,' said Lucille beaming, and she leaned down, giving her mother a quick peck on the cheek. 'Good luck,' she whispered and skipped away to the now grinning Kyle.

'And the cycle repeats,' she said to herself softly.

'As it does,' whispered Lawrence beside her. 'Do you want to go for a walk too?'

Mary looked across the fire at Sophie, whose eyes were watching the two of them and dancing with excitement. She knew Sophie would look after things around here. She nodded, a squeeze in the pit of her stomach as she stood up. They headed in the opposite direction of Lucille and Kyle.

CHAPTER 19

The rock on which they first sat, nearly a year ago, was still warm with the day's sun, but Mary, sitting on it, felt a shiver, and wrapped her arms around herself. She was alone; no, she felt alone. Lawrence had walked to the edge of the water and she sat there contemplating what he had told her. She couldn't imagine losing one of her girls as he had lost his. Just four years old. Meena was her name. She pictured his eyes, filled with tears as he said it. 'Meena.'

It was an accident. A stupid accident, where his wife, Yvonne, had reversed her car into the little girl who had run into its path, crying out for her mother not to leave. Lawrence had seen it all and was not quick enough to stop it from happening. He lived with the guilt, for five years, his marriage had been torn apart and his remaining daughter, Laurie, five at the time, taken away from him.

'She blamed me,' he had said, as they walked side by side. 'Both of them blamed me, and rightfully so. It was my fault. I should have seen it sooner and I should have gotten to her sooner.'

Mary couldn't say anything to relieve his guilt. She wasn't there, but if it were her, she thought, would she have blamed him too? Maybe.

'We were fighting,' he continued. 'We were always fighting. And my little girl didn't want to see her mother leave. But if she stayed it just got worse. Usually, she'd go to her mother's and cool off and come home and it would be good for a few days. It wasn't just her, I had my faults. I should have left sooner. I wasn't good enough for her and we both knew it.'

Mary wondered how this man couldn't be good enough for anyone. He was sensitive and kind, not to mention handsome. And from what she knew about his family, they were well off. He worked for his father's company, a large conglomerate, Patterson and Co, a well-known courier franchise.

'I was in the army, did I tell you that?'

Mary's mind went to Gary and her stomach lurched. She shook her head.

'She wanted me to work for my father,' he said and sniffed cynically. 'Well, I guess I did, but too late. I couldn't go back after the accident. I was a wreck. I took to drinking a lot.' He sighed heavily. 'Well, my marriage ended, and I ended up in a rehabilitation facility. I came out to find my wife and daughter gone.'

'Where?'

'France. To stay with her family there.'

'But how could she have taken your child away without your permission?'

'When one is in rehab, there's not a lot one can do. I tried to get them back. I enlisted the help of my father and we tried everything. I even went there and she allowed me to see Laurie, who told me she didn't want to see me anymore. My six-year-old child, telling her father she didn't want to see him.' He bent his head and Mary looked the other way, understanding he didn't want her to see his distress.

Mary thought of Marina. She hoped she would come out of whatever she was going through. 'That's sad,' she muttered, not able to recall any words that were appropriate for this revelation.

'And that's about it,' he said, breathing a sigh of relief.

'What happened after that? Did you see them again?'

'No, I've written letters, I send cards for birthdays and occasions, but there is never a response. I will keep doing it forever, but I know I can never have them back. Yvonne, I stopped loving a long time ago, even before the accident, we both knew we rushed into the marriage. But my child, I think about her every day, and I dream about her every night.'

'Do you want more children, Lawrence?' said Mary and bit her tongue at her insensitive question. She didn't know what made her ask it; perhaps because he was young, he may want to start another family. She knew she didn't want more children; besides, she was past that, having too much on her plate as it was. 'Sorry,' she said and looked at his face to decipher his thoughts.

He laughed cynically. 'No, I don't. It's too hard, too heartbreaking to think about it.'

Mary looked at the night sky, stars shimmering from it, and watched him standing, stock still, the silhouette of a broken man against the moon. After Lawrence had told her about his life, he had walked towards the water and she remained on the rock, letting him have a moment on his own. She could tell that it was the first time he had shared this story so openly to anyone. She had also wanted a moment to herself, to process what he had just said, to think about her own loss, something she had tried to think less about lately, and it seemed to pale in comparison to his. One husband, as wonderful as he was, against his wife and both his daughters. She couldn't imagine not seeing her girls even for a day. She didn't even know how to comfort him; nothing she could say would be of any comfort. The man had to live with his demons, but she could at least show that she could be there for him.

She slid off the rock and stood behind him. 'I'm sorry,' she said and squeezed his hands that were clasped tightly behind his back. He turned and gave her a lopsided smile, and they both walked back to the party in silence.

****

'Where did you go?' slurred Virginia, who was sitting in Lawrence's seat when they got back to the bonfire. Lawrence had nodded politely to the party and headed into the house. Mary understood that he had just poured out his heart and needed to be by himself.

'For a walk,' said Mary, who really didn't have the energy to put up with Virginia right now. She looked towards Sophie, who was staring back with some concern. She gave her a reassuring smile, but she could tell Sophie wasn't convinced.

'With Lawrence?' asked Virginia.

'Uh-huh.'

'What did you talk about?'

'Not much,' she replied. She was certainly not going to share what Lawrence had told her to anyone, least of all Virginia.

'Do you guys have a thing?' Virginia said a little too loudly, gulping the rest of her glass of whiskey.

'Really, Virginia?'

'No, really, Mary. Virgin Mary.' She cackled with derision.

'I think you may have had a little too much to drink,' said Mary, becoming irritated with the woman's behaviour. But she knew it was never the right thing to say to anyone who was intoxicated.

Virginia pulled herself to a stand with some effort and put her face so close to Mary's she could smell her breath. 'Did you know I slept with Gary?' she said, little bubbles of spit landing on Mary's face.

Mary recoiled. She thought she hadn't heard right. 'What was that?'

'I slept with your husband.' Virginia put her hands on her hips and gnashed her teeth in a malicious smile.

'Go to bed, Virginia.' Mary felt heat rise in her cheeks.

'Yes, the precious man who you put on a pedestal. You think Lawrence wants you? I know he will discard you in a second.' She snapped her fingers, her spittle landing on Mary's nose.

Mary wiped at her nose, trying to keep her cool and thought it weird how some things can become so clear when one is faced with the truth of someone. Virginia was never going to change, to become a better person, a person Mary thought she had inside her, a caring person who was trying to crawl out of that loathsome exterior. She always was and still was the same spiteful, hateful human being, and now Mary suddenly realised her mistake.

'I will need you out of here tomorrow,' said Mary, gritting her teeth. Her fists balled and all she could think about was punching a hole in this woman's face. A normally pretty face that was contorted and showed her true ugliness.

'Out of this hellhole? Sure. I'm over all of you useless people.' She looked over to the Davises. 'Those old goats, who have one foot each in the grave, that wannabe movie star ...' She looked towards Sophie and did a lopsided twirl and turned to Moira. 'Oh, and the riff-raff that come in here ...'

'Like you?' said Mary, her face now hot with fury. Insulting Mary was one thing, she was used to Virginia doing that, but to offend others, people who had put up with her nonsense for the last few weeks, was too much, and Mary felt her heart burst from her chest with anger.

Virginia paused for a second, shocked to hear the words come out of Mary's mouth. Cool, collected and never rude Mary. She took a step towards Mary, her hands raised in readiness to push her, when she suddenly found herself on the sand. The music had stopped and Sophie stood beside Mary, her teeth bared.

'Get out of here, you stupid cow. You have sucked enough out of this woman already, and all of us too. Get out.'

'She can stay the night,' said Mary softly, knowing Virginia was too drunk to drive anywhere, and she knew there wasn't anywhere for her to go. She could organise something the next day.

Virginia still lay on the sand, her scared but defiant eyes moving between Mary to Sophie, and Mary stared back firmly. She was not going to feel sorry for her anymore. She had gone too far.

'I'll take her to her room,' said Natalie, trying to help an objecting Virginia off the sand. Russell came to help and they both took away a mumbling Virginia to her room. Mary flopped herself on the seat Virginia had vacated and put her head in her hands.

'What a bitch,' said Sophie. 'I'm glad you finally told her to leave.' She rubbed Mary's back, which Mary found irritating but also comforting. 'Why did you? What did she say?'

'Nothing,' replied Mary and looked up at the bonfire, which was now sitting in the middle of the pit by itself, everyone at the party slowly heading inside. Only Moira, her scared eyes on them, remained and Mary smiled at her. She smiled back shakily and set about picking up the chairs that were strewn all over the sand.

'Where is everyone?' Lucille and Kyle were coming towards them. 'You bunch of losers.' She laughed. 'You're all too old to party past nine?'

'Big day tomorrow,' said Mary, standing up to help Moira tidy up.

'Really? Why?'

'Virginia's leaving,' said Sophie with a pump of her fist in the air.

125

Lucille laughed. 'About time,' she said, rolling her eyes.

Once everything had been cleared and Kyle had been bid goodbye by a wistful Lucille, Mary walked to the water, trying to fathom what Virginia had said. Could it be true? And if so, when did it happen? Sure, Virginia was vindictive and nasty, but she was never a liar. She looked to the stars and thought of Gary, wondering what was happening.

'What did she say?' Sophie was behind her.

Usually Mary was not one to share her thoughts with many people, but she felt like she needed to talk to someone, and of all the adults in the world, she probably trusted Sophie the most. 'She slept with Gary.'

Sophie, the usually chatty Sophie, who had an opinion on everything, was silent, her mouth agape. After a few moments, Mary looked at her. 'She's lying,' said Sophie.

'No, I don't think she is.' Mary knew somehow that Virginia wasn't.

'Did she tell you about it?'

'You didn't give her the chance.' Mary chuckled involuntarily, as she pictured Virginia lying flat on the ground. She cleared her throat, her mind feeling a sudden sense of calm. 'And I don't want to know more.'

'Why not?' demanded Sophie.

'Because I will always love him, no matter what.' She said it more confidently than she felt. Of course she wanted to know more, but how would that help?

'Yes, but the thought of that woman having one up on

you,' she said, grating her teeth.

'Have you seen her? She doesn't have one up on anyone. She is a sad, lonely woman, who lost everything she had because of who she is.'

'I guess, but some payback would be good,' insisted Sophie.

'Well, I did kick her out.'

'And you're probably already feeling sorry for her,' said Sophie.

She wasn't wrong. Mary was already wondering how Virginia would cope with nowhere to stay, nowhere to go. 'Come on, a big day tomorrow.'

Sophie scrunched up her face. 'Yes, I guess you're enlisting me to help you prepare her room.'

'You got it,' said Mary and put her arm around Sophie, walking back to the house with her friend.

Mary spent some time tidying up things in the house that were not messy, fluffed pillows, moved around ornaments, pulled the rug tight on the floor, anything to keep her out here, rather than going to her room to be alone with her thoughts.

'Night, Mary,' said Mrs Davis.

'Goodnight,' she replied, looking up at the couple who were heading to their room. Mr Davis tipped his cap at her.

'Have a good night, Mary,' said Natalie, popping her head into the lounge. 'Virginia is out cold.'

'Sorry about the party,' said Mary.

'Oh no, we had a great time.' Natalie waved her hands about. 'Lots of dancing and lots of drama!'

Mary raised her eyebrows and shrugged. 'Goodnight, you two.' She continued trying to find something to do. Too much had been said tonight and she needed to compartmentalise it all, but she wasn't ready. Her head was spinning and keeping herself busy was keeping her sane right now.

'Can I help you?' Mary looked up to see Moira standing in the doorway, leaning against the wall.

'No, that's fine,' Mary replied. 'But thanks. Go on to bed, Moira. Goodnight.' The girl dithered for a moment and hurried away.

An hour later, Mary was rearranging the cutlery drawer and when a stainless steel spoon clattered to the floor, she realised she was probably making more noise than she should have been at that time of night, especially when the rest of the house was dead quiet. She closed the drawer, picked up the spoon and placed it in the sink. She might as well go to bed, she would have to be up in a few hours anyway. On her way to bed, knowing she would not be sleeping, she picked which issue was the most important to reflect on.

CHAPTER 20

Mary hadn't slept all night, as she suspected she wouldn't. At first, it was denial. No, it couldn't have happened. She would have known and Gary would never have done that. He loved her too much and she had never seen him lay eyes on another woman in all their time together. But a sick feeling began to form in the pit of her stomach. She knew his moods, how erratic they were, how he could change from one person into someone totally different within a second. But Virginia? How and when? She knew she was never going to ask Virginia about it. She had too much pride to do that. And then it dawned on her. The night before he killed himself. He'd had a couple of drinks and they had been at the piano.

'Play it again,' he whispered in her ear.

'Aren't you sick of it?' Mary herself was sick of it. Listening to 'When a Man Loves a Woman', over and over again. She played while he sang, so close to her ear, his voice grating, cracking with passion, and it used to make her toes curl, but she knew he was going to turn. She could sometimes sense when his moods took over and she knew she was unable to control it. She'd tried teasing, placating, moving him from one space to another, but it never worked. 'Let's go to bed,' she said when the song was done.

'No, again,' he said and leaned his head on her shoulder.

Mary turned towards him and lifted his chin. She kissed him on his lips and ran her hand up his leg. 'Just one more time,' he said and the way he looked at her gave her the shivers. Even after ten years and two children, he could do that to her. She felt herself warm and played the song again.

She stood up and closed the lid of the piano when the song was finished, knowing it was already too late to be making a racket, but his face grew hurt. His eyebrows pushed together and his mouth twisted in pain. How Mary wished she could help him, to understand what happened to him when he became this way. She was never afraid of him but she hurt for him, she could feel his agony, his confusion, and was unable to help, which made her heart cry for him.

'I need to go out,' he said, and Mary nodded. Perhaps a walk on the beach would do him some good. Some cool, fresh air would shake him out of his mood. She knew that it wouldn't happen, that he would come to bed in the early hours, having spent the night on the porch. She'd tried to stay with him in the beginning, but it was clear he didn't want her there, to witness him in the state he was in. She nodded and went in to check on the girls before she retired to their room.

It was past three in the morning when she heard him come in. She remembered because he had tripped on something and it echoed in the silent house and she jumped and felt for him beside her. When she realised he wasn't home yet, she looked immediately at the clock: 3:12 a.m. He sat on the bed and pulled off his clothes but leaned into himself, his head lowered, and Mary folded back the blanket for him to come into. She could smell the whiskey all over him and wondered how he had stayed out on the porch for so long. He hadn't taken the car; she would have heard the engine when he drove out and back in the carpark.

He lay back on the bed and stared at the ceiling. Mary snuggled towards him but he didn't respond.

'Can I help?' she said when she saw a tear glisten in the corner of his eye. He shook his head. Mary put a hand on his cheek and he squeezed his eyes and the tear slid down his temple. She could feel her chest tighten with that same helpless feeling and took her hand back, but before she could, she felt his grip it.

He turned his body towards hers, his eyes creased with pain. 'Tell me you will always love me.'

Mary squeezed his hand. 'All my life,' she said without hesitation.

'No, I mean, no matter what.'

'What do you mean?' Mary asked, wondering what this was all about. He became like this sometimes, so needy, but it was never something that put her off him. Her heart gave a panicked beat. 'What did you do, Gary?' she said slowly. 'Did something happen?'

'Just tell me no matter what you hear, no matter what has happened, that you will never stop loving me.'

'What happened?'

'Nothing happened,' he said, trying to smile, and kissed her lips, leaving them lingering on hers for a few moments. 'Just try to understand me. I know it's hard, but please remember that I love you with every fibre of my being and that will never change.'

Mary tucked her head into his chest, her own pumping with a fear she hadn't felt before.

And now, as she lay in that same bed, staring at the same ceiling he had all those years ago, it began to dawn on her. He wasn't just talking about ending his life the next day, he was talking about what he had done, and her heart constricted with pity and anger.

How could you have done that to me, Gary? She stiffened, trying not to wake the girls with her sobs. *Virginia? Was that it? Was that what drove you to do what you did? No, you were headed that way; I couldn't see it then, but I see it now. How could I have not helped you in some way? You were my life; I would have given my own to make you happy, but I couldn't.* She let a sob escape her mouth.

'Mum, are you okay?' Lucille whispered from the bed below.

Mary hung her hand over the bed and touched her daughter's shoulder. 'I'm fine,' she whispered.

'Do you need me to sleep up there with you?'

'I'm okay, darling,' she said and Lucille took her hand.

She thought of Virginia now, the woman who had always tried to hurt her; why, she never knew. It had begun early in high school when Mary had unwittingly trusted Virginia, confiding in her about her parents when she was in a particularly fragile state. Her father had come home from work, pushed her aside, and her mother, who barely noticed she was in the same house as them, had picked up her bag and they both strolled out of the house, laughing and talking. Mary didn't exist in their world, and even though she knew things could be a lot worse, she felt alone all the time.

Virginia had held her hand and nodded sympathetically, and Mary thought she had finally found a friend she could trust, someone who didn't judge her as everyone else seemed to. But the next day, there were stares and whispers, more so than usual, and a guilty-looking Virginia had avoided her. Mary had forgiven her, but the impact of that shame, for a fifteen-year-old, was more than she could bear. She trusted no one after that, not until she arrived on the steps of Mrs Davis asking for piano lessons.

And all this time, Virginia had known what she had done. Mary could now recall snippets of conversation where Virginia seemed about to confess something, but Mary had never once suspected. Jealousy was a wretched thing and now Mary finally admitted to herself that was what Virginia felt about her. From as far back as high school when Mary grew into herself, and when Gary had chosen to spend the rest of his life with Mary and dismissed Virginia as if she didn't exist.

Mary sighed. Well, that had changed somewhere. And the last straw for Virginia was when she was rebuffed by Lawrence because it was clear he didn't have eyes for anyone but Mary. And it was in Virginia's low state, when she needed attention, when she had been discarded by her husband, needing someone to find her special. And once again, Mary had taken what she believed should have been hers.

Mary considered what she had just thought. Was it time to admit how she felt for him? And how he felt for her? She should have seen it earlier, been straight with herself, instead of avoiding the obvious. Perhaps she could have dealt with things better. But what was she going to do? Throw herself at him? She was not the type to do that. And the alternative was … She didn't know.

But she couldn't deal with thoughts of Lawrence right now. Her head was aching and she looked at the clock on her bedside table, which showed 2.34. She shivered and got out of bed, wrapped her shawl around her shoulders and went to the kitchen, made herself a cup of tea and went out to the porch. She sat on the armchair and stared into the dark night, the only sound the lapping of the water against the sand.

CHAPTER 21

It had been a busy Saturday, which suited Mary just fine. Lawrence and Sophie helped ready the girls' room to move them back into, but the moment they began to shift the set of drawers back, a call came in asking for a room for a night. Natalie and Russell's room was already booked for guests so the room Virginia had vacated would be needed. Lucille screwed up her face and Marina shrugged.

'One more night,' she promised them. 'He was stuck and practically begged. I won't take any more boarders until we have empty rooms from now on, okay?' Lucille smiled happily and took out the washing.

Virginia had left before breakfast; Mary heard her car slink away just after dawn broke and Mary was relieved she didn't have to face her. Her head still hurt from thinking and the lack of sleep. She made a strong cup of coffee when she saw the sun rise over the horizon and set her mind to the day ahead. There was no point looking to the past anymore, not for answers, not for anything. She ducked back into the house when she heard Lawrence stir, as he did early every morning.

After lunch, she booked in the new arrivals, a couple of girls in their twenties from Melbourne who were passing through on their way to Adelaide. They were a chatty twosome who, after they dumped their backpacks in the room, headed straight out to enjoy the sights, not returning until late that evening. By then Mary, Lucille and Sophie had cleaned the rooms, done the washing and had dinner ready. The other lone traveller came in just before dinner and went straight to his room, thanking them for taking him on such late notice.

Tonight everyone asked for dinner and Mary was only too happy to oblige, glad for the distraction.

'Are you okay?' Sophie asked when she found Mary alone in the kitchen, her eyes gazing out into shimmering evening sky. Mary had surrounded herself with the guests all day, chattering happily with the Davises, joking with the girls while they helped with the chores and laughing with Sophie, who knew better than to try to bring up anything of the previous night, knowing her friend wanted to keep her mind active with insignificant things. But now Mary had caught a glimpse of the ocean through the window and her skin tingled, her heart tight. Maybe she had to leave here, escape this place and the constant reminders of the man she loved, the same man who was tortured and ten years after his passing, had hurt her.

'I'm okay,' said Mary wearily.

'She's gone. She can't hurt you.'

'She didn't,' replied Mary, not turning around, still looking into the abyss.

Sophie put her arms around Mary and leaned her head on her back. 'I've got you. You know that, right?'

That's when Mary felt a tear well and she clutched at Sophie's hands. 'I know that.'

'Let's do this,' Lucille said loudly. 'I've recruited help.'

Mary turned around and looked at Lucille, who gave her a wink. She smiled in thanks, not just for the help but she could see her intuitive daughter knew that she needed to be around people to keep her mind away from something. Usually the Davises, Sophie and Lawrence, and before tonight, Virginia, chipped in with dinner, each taking turns to buy the groceries and cooking for all. It was like a little family and Mary was happy that this little tradition continued. Today even Moira joined them and Mary was happy to have the little waif coming more out of her shell. She had a feeling Moira would be here for a while. The music was turned on and even Marina seemed in a good mood, but perhaps that was because Lawrence, who she stuck close to, was helping out. Mary shook her head. She may as well have left dinner on the menu, but she was not unhappy about it at all, especially tonight when she felt the love and care that was shown by the people around her.

She looked furtively at Lawrence, who had not tried to talk to her about anything in particular. When he came out in the morning, he helped with breakfast as he usually did and then disappeared for the day. He had barely spoken to her all day and hadn't enquired about Virginia's absence. He got back just before the dinner preparations began and when it was done and set out on the table, the little party sat happily at the table.

'This is so much better,' said Sophie and no one asked to what she was referring. 'A toast,' she said and raised her glass. 'To goodbyes. Forever goodbyes.' She smiled cheekily and sipped at her wine.

Lucille smiled but Lawrence was staring at Mary, who realised she was frowning. She quickly opened her mouth in a grin and he offered her a crooked one. She felt Sophie's leg nudge her under the table and gave it a little kick back.

When dinner was finished and everyone had

congratulated themselves on a job well done, Lucille and Sophie helped with the washing and drying while Lawrence cleared the table. Marina disappeared to her room.

'Can I go out for a bit?' Lucille asked with hope in her eyes.

'With?'

'Kyle.' Lucille smiled shyly.

'Where is he?'

'Outside. He's been waiting since before dinner.'

'Oh Lucille! You should have asked him to come in.'

'No. I'm glad he waited.'

Mary felt a growing admiration for her elder daughter. She knew what she was doing, how to deal with boys, and she knew she couldn't be steered wrong.

'Go on. Not too late, okay? It's getting dark.'

'Thanks, Mum,' said Lucille and giving her mother a quick hug, she skipped out the door.

'Are you okay?' whispered Sophie again.

'I'm okay,' Mary replied. She wasn't so sure, but not thinking about it all had helped. The evening was passed watching a movie with the Davises, Sophie and Moira, and when it was finished, just after eight thirty, Sophie yawned, deciding to have an early night after the late one the night before. It was the Davises' bedtime anyway and Moira perched herself on the sofa to watch a show by herself.

Mary left her to go to the porch to wait for Lucille to return. She sat in the old, used armchair, the one Gary had loved but she had hated, old and brown, but soft and comfy. Now she was alone, Gary's face swam before her and her eyes began to sting. She squeezed them tight and tried to remember the joy she had with him, the laughter, the love, the absolute devotion. Maybe not so much devotion on his part. She hated herself for that thought. He was obviously a sick man, and even she couldn't get through to him.

'Are you really waiting for me, Mum?' Lucille's voice drifted up the stairs.

'I'm still your mother. How was your evening?'

'Good,' she said her eyes glazing over. 'He's so dreamy.'

'They are the ones you have to worry about,' said Mary with a chuckle.

'Hmmm. Can I invite him over one day? Like you know, for dinner or something?'

'That serious?' Mary was surprised.

'Maybe, I think so.'

'Okay, how about tomorrow? Sunday roast?'

'Sounds great. Thanks, Mum.' Lucille planted a kiss on her mother's forehead and bounced into the house.

Mary smiled to herself. Lucille was nearly an adult. Soon she would be gone. She'd already applied for nurse's training in Melbourne, and it would mean she would have to move there. There was no way she was going to travel all the way from this place. She worried about her but she also knew Lucille had a good head on those tough shoulders. It was Marina that Mary worried about now, but since Lawrence had been staying here, Marina had shown her face outside of the bedroom much more often.

The cold of the evening and way too much iced tea made her bladder pinch and she went inside the house. On her way back through the hallway, she spotted the piano and stopped. She ran her finger over the light layer of dust on the lid and felt her body shake. She opened it and saw the keys gleam up at her. She set herself down on the seat and rested her fingers on them. She depressed her fingertips and a burst nostalgia hit her, but she didn't stop, letting the music guide her, drive her. She was singing in her head, the same song, 'When a Man Loves a Woman', and she could feel him beside her, leaning his head on her shoulder, singing softly into her neck.

She finished the song and removed her hands from the piano, laying them on her lap. She stared at the keys and realised she had survived. Life didn't end when she played, not even *their* song. She heard a movement behind her but she didn't turn around. Her heart was full, a longing for this instrument she never felt she could have again. She knew there was a reason she didn't throw it away but she always thought it was because of Gary, that he wouldn't have liked that. Now she knew it was because of her. Because she loved it. She closed the lid and went back out onto the porch.

She pulled her shawl around her and turned the ring on her finger round and round. She still remembered his face so clearly …

'Penny for your thoughts?'

Mary spun around to see Lawrence standing at the door. She hadn't even heard it open and it looked like he'd been standing there for a while. 'Not worth that much,' she replied and involuntarily smoothed the stray strands of hair that had been blowing in the breeze.

'Need some company?'

Mary was surprised. Lawrence had never outwardly sought her company before. They always seemed to just bump into each other, even though she realised lately it was no accident. She nodded and he dragged another chair to where she sat.

'Too late for a stroll?'

Mary was tempted, but it was late and she knew what those temptations meant, and right now she was mixed up, thoughts of Gary rolling around in her head. She had not even stopped for a second to contemplate what Lawrence had told her yesterday and she felt guilty. For that matter, she hadn't even given herself the chance to think about what she felt for Lawrence. 'Maybe too late,' she replied and looked towards the sea, not wanting to witness his reaction. 'Would you like some tea? I just got a new batch of peppermint tea. I could use a cup of chocolate myself. Or would you prefer chocolate?'

'The tea is fine,' he said.

She made the tea and chocolate and came back out, handing him his cup.

'Do you want to talk about it?' he asked.

'No ... I don't know.' She was shocked that came out. She had barely had a decent conversation with this man apart from yesterday, but she couldn't deny the chemistry she felt when she was near him. It seemed like the hairs on her arms had already stood on end and from the moment he stepped out on the porch, all thoughts of Gary had disappeared clear out of her mind. Now she was tempted to talk to him about it?

'You can talk to me, you know.'

She nodded and almost felt obliged to tell him about her woes, as he did with her yesterday. 'Just something Virginia said.'

He sniffed but didn't reply.

'How do you know someone loves you? Like, you know, truly loves you?'

'There are many forms of love, I guess. Parental love …'

She rolled her eyes. 'Don't get philosophical on me. You know the love I mean.'

'I guess you never really know if you're loved. Only the person who loves knows. The other believes or chooses to believe or chooses not to believe.'

'That's heavy. In that case, do people just fool themselves?'

'It's called self-preservation. You have to choose to believe. That way you have some purpose in life, because, let's face it, it's what life is made of.'

'I don't know if that's the most romantic thing I've ever heard or the most cynical.' Mary laughed, suddenly feeling very easy with Lawrence.

'Maybe a bit of both.' He looked at her. 'Tell me about him.'

Mary sighed. 'In a second, everything I thought was real was bent, screwed up.'

'Because of Virginia?' Mary nodded and he raised his eyebrows. 'You must learn to discern the motives of people.'

'I know who she is, what she's like, but I also wanted to believe she could be a good person. And maybe she is …'

'She's not a nice woman.'

'What did she say to you?' Mary was curious as to how Virginia had come on to him.

He reddened. 'She was pretty straightforward, I'll give her that.'

'Were you surprised?'

'I guess, but I also saw how she was and honestly, I tried to avoid her.'

Mary laughed again. 'So you saw her strut around in her teeny-weeny togs and knew her game all along.'

He blew out a loud breath. 'I've been here for more than two weeks, so I finally gathered.'

'So, I'm curious. Why did you reject her?'

'And miss that walk with you?' He raised his voice in mock exaggeration and gestured to the beach. 'Where I got the chance to show you the true man I am?'

Mary wasn't sure if he was joking anymore. 'Lawrence, I am grateful that you trusted me enough to share that with me.'

He leaned forward, his face close to hers. 'You didn't judge me? Think I'm a terrible person for what I did?'

'You didn't mean to do anything,' she replied and leaned

away from him. 'Do you want some more tea?'

'Tell me about what happened.'

'There's nothing to tell,' she replied and turned from him. Right now, she didn't want to be reminded of Gary.

'Are you in love with another man?'

She spun to face him. 'What? No!'

'Why do you avoid me?'

She didn't even know where to begin. The plethora of emotions she felt when she was near him, the change in her very being when he was in the same room, the tingles she felt in the pit of her stomach when he spoke to her. Her heart was already beating so fast and so loud, she could swear he could hear it. 'I don't know.'

He reached his hand forward and moved a strand of hair from her forehead, letting it linger along the side of her cheek. She let it stay there, her eyes locked on his. She could see his want, his need for her, a reflection of her own desire. She closed her eyes and felt his face near hers, the graze of his lips on hers.

She jerked back her head. 'I'm sorry,' she squealed and bolted back into the house, into the comfort of her bedroom.

****

Another sleepless night lay ahead as Mary tossed and turned. It was barely three a.m. when she got up, realising there would be no sleep tonight either. Maybe she could do some of her paperwork. It had been piling up and she had kept putting it off.

She turned on the kettle and stood by it, waiting for it to boil. She leaned on the sink and looked out at the night. It was still now, barely a wave on the ocean, just a gentle lapping of the water on the shore. She smiled. Just the thing she needed. She turned off the kettle and pulled the blanket that sat near the door, over her shoulders, and went out into the night. She stood at the edge of the water as she always did when she needed to feel calm and it was working.

'Can't sleep either?' Lawrence was behind her but she didn't turn around.

'Do you want to be by yourself?'

She shook her head.

'I'm sorry ... about before.'

She shook her head again and didn't flinch when his arms wrapped around her. His breath was on her neck and it seemed the most natural thing in the world, this feeling of terror, and excitement and want. She turned into him and let him put his lips on hers.

CHAPTER 22

Mary allowed him to kiss her, his lips warm and soft, and she let herself be held by Lawrence, clinging to him, feeling things she hadn't felt in a long time. Gary was not in her thoughts, not now. She knew this was not Gary, this was Lawrence, brooding, wary Lawrence, who held her as if his life depended on it. She felt the blanket slip down to the sand as she wrapped her arms around his neck, the touch of his skin warm and smooth. He pulled her closer and she didn't want to ever let go, but he reared his head back at her and stared into her eyes.

'You know, you have the most beautiful eyes I've ever seen.'

'No,' she replied. 'You do.' She chuckled. 'That's a line from a movie, I'm sure.'

'Do you want to take a walk?' he asked, looking back at the house. If anyone were to look out the window, there wouldn't be much denying what was happening, she realised, surprised she had let herself forget for a moment that the real world existed, one where she wasn't ready to be with another man.

She nodded and picked up her blanket. She wasn't feeling cold anymore and she reached for his hand. 'Clouds have come in,' she said, looking at the starless sky. 'Rain will come soon, maybe not tonight, maybe tomorrow.' She didn't care if it rained or didn't, Mary just couldn't think of anything logical to say. She felt like a teenager on a first date. But this man by her side didn't feel like any teenager she had ever kissed, not that she had kissed many.

They walked for a while in silence and Lawrence suddenly stopped. 'I'm sorry,' he said.

Mary turned to him, surprised. 'Sorry? For what?' Then she understood. 'Are you sorry?'

'No. I'm just sorry if I've made your life more complicated.'

'No, not complicated.' She didn't know what she felt. Elation? Ecstasy? 'I don't know how I'll feel tomorrow.'

'I could be gone by then if you want.' His eyes told her that wasn't what he wanted.

'If you need to,' she shrugged nonchalantly. She wasn't feeling nonchalant at all. 'Do you want to kiss me again?'

'You have no idea how much I've wanted to kiss you every day. From the moment I laid eyes on you.'

'And yet you didn't.'

He put his palm on her cheek and drew her in again. And when he kissed her, she hoped he would never leave, ever. She dropped to her knees and he followed, his mouth finding the lobes of her ears, his fingers drawing the sleeve off her shoulder, and she clung to his arms, feeling the pull of his muscles, taut with his need for her. When she felt his bulge against her thigh, she felt a pang of fear, of guilt, and reared away from him.

'I'm sorry,' he said, his head bent in remorse.

Mary ran her fingers through the thick mop in front of her. 'Just don't let's ruin this.' She wanted him to keep going, to feel every inch of him. Every particle in her body tingled, like little pins pricking the skin, and it hurt but it felt wonderful. A year of imagining, or trying not to imagine this, was too much for her to take in one night. Lawrence rolled over onto his back and took her hand. She lay beside him, leaving her hand in his, and gazed at the sky.

'Maybe we should go back,' he said.

'Can we stay here for a while?'

'Uh-huh,' he replied, and she could hear the smile in his voice.

It seemed perfect. The cool night, the sparkling stars that had crept out from behind the clouds, the tension in the air, her hand nestled in his palm. 'All my life,' she began. Lawrence shifted to move the blanket over her bare shoulder. 'You get sick of it sometimes, you know,' she said, almost to herself. 'You are this person, and everyone expects you to be this person. The perfect wife, the perfect mother, the perfect everything. And it's expected, because you can't be anything else but that.' Her mouth watered. She'd never voiced this to anyone before, had never even admitted it to herself. 'And sometimes, you just don't want to be that. You just want to be, I don't know, bad. Selfish.'

Lawrence didn't reply but she could see from the corner of her eye his chest rise and fall heavily.

'But you can't be bad because you let people down, you disappoint them, but every inch of you wants to feel what it is to do something ...'

Lawrence turned onto his side, lifting his head and resting it in his palm. 'What do you want to do, Mary? You, not anyone else, you.'

She turned to him, his eyes asking for her truth, daring her to say it. 'You're not the "bad" I mean, Lawrence, but I want you.'

'You have me,' he replied and put his lips on hers again.

The tingles turned to pricks, the sensation moving all the way down to her toes, and she pulled him to her. 'Then let me be bad tonight.'

****

'I have to go back next week,' said Lawrence.

They were both sitting on their rock, far away from prying eyes, his arm around her waist, her head buried in his chest. 'I know,' she replied, but her heart still fell. It had been a week since he had come to her on the beach and made love to her and she hoped that maybe he would now stay a little longer.

'At least you won't have to hide from everyone when I walk into the room,' he said and chuckled. It had been difficult trying to keep their emotions from rising when they walked into the same room and if others were around, they couldn't even look at each other, fearful that others would sense the new dynamic between them. Sophie, Mary was sure, knew already, and she admired the strength it would have taken her not to say anything about it.

'Where did you go?' Mary asked Lawrence now.

'When?'

'When you didn't come back for half a year.'

He turned from her and threw a rock into the water. 'I didn't want to come back.'

Mary stiffened. 'Why not?'

'Because it was hard to. Because my mind was in turmoil. Because I couldn't stand to be around you.'

'Why not?' asked Mary, knowing why. It had been the same with her.

'I went away for a while. To France. To see them. To see if I could be a part of their lives again.'

'Oh,' said Mary, disappointed with his response.

He turned to her now. 'I thought my head was going in the wrong direction. That my infatuation with you was because of the crazy stuff with my family.'

'What happened in France?' She wondered why he hadn't told her about this part when he bared his soul to her more than a week ago.

'After seeing you with Marina and Lucille, I just wanted to see if they were ready to forgive me. They were not. I saw them. They saw me. Across the street with another man.' He shrugged but Mary saw the veins on the skin of his throat stretch. 'They turned away, both of them. I waited for my daughter to turn back, to see me, and to have some care, maybe a spark of forgiveness, but she didn't.'

'What did you do?'

He laughed. 'I came back immediately and spent the next five and a half months pining for you, waiting for a call.' He frowned at her. 'You never called.'

'No, I didn't. What was I supposed to say? Come over, dear Lawrence, sweep me away to another life?' She laughed and he laughed back, tapping her on the nose.

'No, but I would have been here in a second,' he said as he snapped his fingers.

'You're here now,' she said, resting her head on his shoulder.

'I couldn't stay away. I am a weak man,' he said, kissing her forehead. 'For you I am weak.'

'That makes both of us,' she replied, thinking of her weakness that night when her head was in turmoil and her fight to keep her feelings inside her. But since that night when she gave in to herself, and to Lawrence, her mind was free. She woke up every morning with a whistle on her lips and a twinkle in her eye, and when she tried to think about Virginia and what she had said, she scolded herself. The woman was not worth it. Whatever happened was well in the past and she was free of the past. It was up to her to understand that and now she did. Gary still swam in her brain in unguarded moments, but she didn't dwell on him as she used to.

For the first time since Gary died, Mary's future looked bright. And yes, it was Lawrence, but it wasn't just him, it was the realisation that she could have a future without Gary, that she could love and be loved back, that love for her wasn't reserved for her dead husband. And even if things didn't work for them, she had hope for herself, not just for her children, but for herself, and for the first time, she didn't feel guilty or selfish to wish for more.

She smiled as she thought back to that night when she

finally succumbed to what she had been feeling, how it had been so wonderful, her body rising to the challenge, something she hadn't felt in so long, an awakening of all her senses. And he had been tender, assertive, yet patient. She could see his need when she looked into his eyes, which gazed back with a fierce love. And when they were spent, they wrapped themselves in each other and lay in their warmth, Mary not wanting to return to the house. But the chill of the night was too much to bear even against the warm of his skin and Mary, snuggling her stockinged feet into the crook of Lawrence's knees, knew they would turn to icicles if they stayed out here too long.

'Maybe we should go back,' he had said softly in her ear.

She nodded, raising herself to a sit and felt him move behind her, shivering when she felt his lips on her back. She remained in that position for a moment and forced herself to stand up, straightening her clothes and wrapping her shawl back around her shoulders. They wandered back slowly and in silence, each lost in their own thoughts, an awkwardness growing now after their intense passion just moments earlier.

'Are you okay, Mary? I can leave tomorrow if this is uncomfortable for you.'

Mary thought about it. She didn't know what she was feeling. But uncomfortable seemed to be the perfect word right now. How would things be tomorrow, or the day after? What if he didn't want her after tonight? What if she didn't want him? Things could look gravely different from what they did now. She didn't reply. She didn't know how. When they reached the house, he kissed her cheek.

'Don't go tomorrow,' she said and went to her room.

****

But now, a week later, he was going. For how long she didn't know and dared not ask. She didn't want to be disappointed if he told her he couldn't return soon. If he told her he would return and didn't, she would have to bear even more heartbreak. It had been a perfect week, late evenings spent with Lawrence, walking in the moonlight, talking and kissing, but it hadn't gone any further and as much as Mary wanted it to, she couldn't let it happen again. If he loved her, he would understand. And he never pushed for more, as much as his body told her he wanted it.

'I'm going to leave before daybreak,' he said.

Mary nodded. That would probably be best. No moping around, no teary goodbyes, trying to hide from the world her distress. She knew well how to bottle it in and hold it until she was alone. But now, her heart hurt, her chest was tight.

'This has honestly been the best week of my life.' He kissed her shoulder. 'You made me forget, and you made me remember.'

'Me too,' she said and turned away, trying to keep the tear in her eye from spilling down her cheek. How she wanted to ask if he was returning.

CHAPTER 23

Lucille's formal went off perfectly. Kyle shyly asked Mary for permission to accompany Lucille to the event and off they went in his little brown Ford. Mary was reminded that Lucille would soon be going away. She had already been accepted to train as a nurse in Melbourne, even before she completed her exams. And when she came home from the formal, Mary saw an adult before her, ready to begin her life away from Righteous Creek, from her mother and sister. She silently cheered for her daughter, who was so strong, so bold, everything she wanted her to be.

'Have I told you how proud I am of you?' she said when Lucille walked into the lounge room after the formal, her face flushed, her mouth in a beaming smile. Mary had been waiting inside, not wanting Lucille to think she was waiting up for her.

'I think you may have,' Lucille replied and sat down with a flourish on the sofa next to Mary. 'My feet hurt though.'

'Too much dancing will do that.'

Lucille became silent and stared ahead of her, at the photo of her father.

'What is it?' asked Mary, her gaze going to that of her daughter's.

'Dad.' She turned to Mary. 'I still miss him.' Mary nodded. She had tried not to let thoughts of Gary and his final days invade her mind. 'Do you?'

'I do,' replied Mary.

'But you know, Mum, you can move on.' Mary nodded again, less certainly this time. She wondered where this was going, but Lucille straightened her dress and raised herself from the sofa. 'Love you, Mum,' she said, and left the room.

'You haven't told me all about the formal,' called Mary.

Lucille stopped at the door and turned around. 'Tomorrow,' she said. 'I'm zonked. But it was the most wonderful night.'

Mary smiled as she watched Lucille dance away and admired her child, mischievous, straight-talking, confident, and felt a surge of pride and relief knowing the future for her was bright. Marina, on the other hand, was becoming more of a problem. Mary frowned.

A month after Lawrence had left, Marina had gone completely back into her shell and Mary was finding it tough to cope with, constantly trying to coax her out of her room, trying to get her to school on time. This phase was lasting longer than it should have and now, understanding a little more the extent of Gary's mental state, she worried for her. She couldn't very well rely on Lawrence to help bring Marina out of her shell all the time. He was not her father and was certainly not responsible for her state of mind. Lucille helped by dragging Marina out of bed, scolding her and soothing her, but Mary knew she would be gone soon and she felt helpless. Marina wasn't disrespectful or even rebellious. She was just so introverted, so strange, and Mary often caught her staring into space, her eyebrows knitted, her teeth biting down on her lip.

'Hey, Marina,' Mary would call or just walk past and tousle her hair. Marina barely responded and when she did it seemed like irritation that emanated from her, flinching when she felt her mother's touch. She'd now taken to spending most evenings out of the house, getting back from school as late as six. When Mary questioned her, she would shrug and tell her she'd been studying at the library and wouldn't offer any other explanation. Mary tried being tough and demanding Marina be home early but Marina just nodded and came home late the next day again. Mary even tried picking her straight up from school and when she did, Marina reluctantly got into the car and rode home in silence. But on the days Mary was busy and couldn't get to the school on time to pick her up, inevitably, Marina would return home after six.

But in the evenings, when the girls were in the safety of the house, Mary sat on the porch, her thoughts with Lawrence. She didn't want to think, obsess over him, it seemed so childish, but her mind kept returning to him at the most random of moments. In the shower, while cooking breakfast or washing sheets. She let herself think of him when she wandered the beach alone in the moonlight or when she lay in bed and pictured him lying beside her as he did on the sand that first evening.

'Are you missing him?' Sophie asked a few days after Lawrence had left, and Mary had just nodded. 'He will be back,' she said.

Mary nodded again and wondered when that would be. He hadn't said.

'Are you going to tell me about it?'

Mary smiled sheepishly. 'Not yet,' she said. She herself

didn't quite know where things stood between her and Lawrence, and Sophie would just be on her case about it whichever way it went.

The boarding house now held just the Davises, Sophie, who was taking a summer break from work, or so she said, and Moira, who wandered about the place, trying to help out and not be in the way. She had taken to the Davises, who entertained her with stories of their courtship and introduced her to old movies and music. Moira had booked her room indefinitely, but Mary had a feeling it was where she felt safe and at home and now she that she had an income, the first thing she did was pay for her stay. Mary tried to protest, but Moira scuttled away before she could. Apart from Lawrence's room, only one remained free and took in the intermittent visitor, and Mary took to offering breakfast and dinner again. After all, she was doing it for most of the guests anyway and everyone in the house chipped in and helped out with paying for and preparations of the cooking. They were an odd assortment of people, but they were the family they all needed.

Save for one. Lawrence. But hope was fading and Mary began to feel the unfamiliar sense of insecurity. *Was it too soon to have become so involved? One week meant nothing really. Did he have second thoughts after that week? Had he found someone else?* These thoughts pervaded her brain and it was something that took her completely off guard. She had never felt this way before. Not with Gary, not with anyone.

At times she wished they had played the mating dance forever rather than have actually done it. Who was she to mess with a younger man anyway? He had a whole life, some of which she knew nothing about. In three months, she would be forty, and he would be … she didn't even want to think it, it sounded so grimy.

He called her into the third week.

'Missing me?' he asked with a playful lilt in his voice.

Mary didn't know how to answer. 'Um ...' She was a little miffed that it had taken him this long to call.

'Well, I miss you.' He paused. 'I really do.'

Mary softened. 'Why haven't you returned, then?'

'Because it's been ridiculous. I had to drive up to Perth again and then from there, straight to Brisbane. Summer is coming and there is so much to do. Old stock, new stock.' He gave a heavy sigh. 'I am hoping to come down in a few weeks. I hope you will have room for me.'

Mary didn't tell him she kept his room free. She told no one that, but whenever she gave one of the other rooms away, she got a knowing look from Sophie, and even Lucille. Her heart soared at his words but she tried not to get her hopes up. His job was unpredictable, especially at such a busy time as this. Besides, she didn't want to sound too needy. 'Yes, I don't think we're booked for a few weeks, but if someone comes in ...' She left the sentence hanging.

'Who's there now? Anyone who might steal you away from me?'

Mary's heart warmed at that. 'No one who could do that,' she said and the face of Gary floated through her mind. This sounded like a conversation they'd had often, a teasing, playful banter that she now realised was more serious than she'd thought it was at the time.

They talked for a little longer and Mary told him about who had come to the boarding house since he'd left, the strange man who stayed for a week, who'd spent most of his time plucking at the flowers in her garden, the young woman and her son who had stayed for a couple of days and had vacated early in the morning without paying.

'You really should take payment up front,' said Lawrence. 'I could have swindled you on that first night.'

'So you thought about it then, swindling me?'

'I was in love the moment I laid eyes on you.'

Mary was shy now and glad he was on the other end of the phone so he didn't have to see her face flush. 'I have to go,' she said when she heard the bell jangle and looking up, saw a woman in high heels and dark glasses enter. 'A guest,' she said.

'A handsome guest?'

'So very handsome,' she said with a chuckle. 'See you.'

She hung up and realised she hadn't lied. The woman was a beautiful specimen and a twinge of jealousy ran through her; again, a sensation that was so alien to her, she felt ashamed of herself.

She looked down at her baggy skirt, her worn-out sandals and tried to remember how long it had been since she had been shopping or sewn something new for herself. She tried to remember the last item of clothing she'd bought for herself and couldn't. She considered her reflection in the mirror that evening. Yes, she was a good-looking woman, the light creases on the corners of her eyes softening the bigness of her eyes, her broad forehead enhancing her hairline, but she could take more care of herself; not for Lawrence, he seemed to be attracted to her even with her long, ratty hair and naked face.

I'm too old to think about these things, she thought. *They shouldn't matter.* But as she brushed a little of Lucille's compact on her cheeks, she smiled to herself. She missed dressing up as she had when she was younger, when she wanted just a little bit of confidence, a bit of spark to make her feel good about herself. Age was not a reason to have let herself go for so long.

It was a rainy November evening and everyone was scattered around the house. She went into the dining room and found Sophie and Moira playing cards and sat down at the table with them.

'Want to cut in?' asked Sophie, who was having a hell of a time trying to beat Moira at gin. 'I need help.' She narrowed her eyes at Moira. 'She's hustling me.'

'What are you two doing tomorrow?'

'Why?' Sophie sounded dubious.

'Nothing,' said Moira. Mary noticed that she was more talkative than she used to be; her ever present frown always graced her forehead, but her smile came out much more often than it used to.

'I want to go into Melbourne. Shopping,' she said.

'I'm in,' Sophie almost yelped.

'I don't know ...' Moira was more hesitant and Mary knew she didn't have very much cash to spare.

'No expectations. I just need to spruce up my wardrobe.' She ignored Sophie's eyes that were now aimed suspiciously at her. 'Just a day out, the girls. I don't have chores that need doing immediately and I know for a fact you don't have a shift tomorrow, Moira.' Sophie nudged Moira and the girl still didn't look convinced but nodded.

'Great!' Mary said, excited. 'I'll ask Mrs Davis and it's Saturday tomorrow so maybe the girls would like to come too.'

Mrs Davis, who couldn't imagine a more boring day out, politely declined and Marina declined for the same reason. Lucille screwed up her nose.

'Why do you have to do it now? I have exams coming up.'

'You could take a break,' said Mary, but Lucille said it was fine, she couldn't think about shopping anytime soon.

The three women woke early the next day and drove to the city, chatting all the way about what they would buy, where they would go, what they would eat for lunch, a buzz of excitement in the air. And Mary splurged. She could ill afford to waste money, but she let herself do it and even bought two dresses for Moira, who had walked timidly past racks, fingering the pretty clothes, of which she had so few. She also picked up a few books for Marina and a suitcase for Lucille, sorrowful that her daughter would be leaving and coming to the hustle and bustle of this place which seemed so full, so rushed.

Sophie even convinced Mary to cut and style her hair, insisting she would look great with bangs. 'It will highlight those amazing eyes of yours,' she said, and Mary went back to the moment Lawrence had looked into them and admired them. No, she thought, this was their day, a day for fun, a day to pamper themselves, a day to be girls, not a day to get lost in thoughts of Lawrence. But she did heed Sophie's advice, chopping her hair to just below her shoulders, amazed at the lightness of it. She couldn't stop moving her head about, feeling it bounce, and when she walked past a window and caught herself in the reflection, she gasped, barely recognising the attractive, strange woman who was reflected in it.

They came home late, exhausted but elated, and when Mary began to calculate how much she had spent, she scolded herself. It was one day out, something she never did and she was not going to feel guilty about it. She was not going to be that perfect person anymore. She was allowed to live. Her girls were healthy and well looked after, and she put good food on their table every day. She had nothing to feel guilty about. And in the next few days, she found that she enjoyed taking care of herself too, a dash of mascara, a brush of her now luscious hair, outfits that didn't hang from her limbs, but fit her athletic body.

'I knew there was a sexy mama in there somewhere,' said Sophie with a laugh when she came out to breakfast the next morning. Mary was wearing a pair of fitted jeans with a yellow spotted blouse and had even put on the earrings she had bought from the bargain store. 'I'd better watch my back!'

'Oh, stop it, Soph,' said Mary reddening.

'Lady, I think you're gonna snag some guy very soon.'

'I don't want a guy,' said Mary, frowning.

'He will come back, hun,' said Sophie.

CHAPTER 24

Lawrence did come back, just a week later, and Mary was not expecting him at all. She had been strolling the beach as she normally did in the evening, and she had sat on their rock, the warm breeze reminding her of her last night with Lawrence. She didn't want to miss him, and each day it had gotten better; she busied herself with getting things ready for Lucille's departure, but she still thought of him all the time. She didn't feel the same clinging feeling she had for Gary anymore and sometimes she missed it.

Gary had been gone for so long but she'd held onto him for so much longer and wasn't sure she could give him up, at least not the thought of him and not her love for him. She knew that no matter what happened and whoever it happened with, she would love Gary forever. Virginia was of no consequence anymore and the embarrassment of it all had worn off that same night when she realised how sick Gary had been and how the thought of hurting her drove him to the end. She wondered how things might have been if he had told her or even someone else about how he felt rather than have kept everything bottled up inside him. She remembered how the first few years after his death she would go over conversations she should have had with him, what she should have said to make him open up. But it was too late and she consoled herself by living with the ghost of the man that he was when he was loving her.

But since Lawrence had come into her life, she did it less often, her stomach knotting at the thought of him, and she realised now that Lawrence, in some ways, reminded her of her dead husband. The way he looked at her with broody eyes, like she was the only living being in the universe. The way he didn't entertain the attentions of anyone else, the way he gave his full attention to what he felt was important to her, namely the girls.

She laughed to herself now as she swished her hair, so light and fluffy, around her face, thinking about her conversation with Lucille, who was impressed with her mother's new attitude and encouraged her by giving her makeup tips and hints on the new fashions.

'Where is this coming from, Mum?' Lucille had asked one day when Mary was looking for her earrings.

'Where is what coming from?'

'This new look.' She curled one side of her mouth. 'Is it, dare I say, a new man?'

'Don't be silly,' said Mary, waving her away, trying not to allow her face to redden.

'You know it's okay if you're seeing him. He's cool.'

'I'm not …'

'I know, I know,' said Lucille, rolling her eyes. 'But if you are, that would be cool. He's a good guy. And Marina loves him.'

'Stop it, Lu,' said Mary. She wasn't ready to let anyone know about Lawrence and she didn't know if she ever would be.

'Dad would be happy too, I think.' Lucille was twiddling

her fingers together.

'Well, that is of no consequence then, is it? Because I'm not seeing Lawrence and I'm not seeing anyone else.'

She still couldn't bank on his love, no matter how much his actions showed otherwise. What if she lost herself in it all and he suddenly realised he didn't want her anymore? What if he had found someone else in the meantime? Someone younger, sexier. With more in common with him than her, a middle-aged mother who lived in the middle of nowhere. The same insecurities kept rising to the surface and she had to keep reminding herself that he said he would come back and she had to trust that he would. And if he didn't, well, she had lived a good life before he came into it, one that she felt safe in.

'Oh Lawrence,' she said softly, hugging her knees as she stared into the ocean; so lost was she in her thoughts that she was oblivious to the call of her name. People were still on the beach at nine in the evening, summer giving way to much longer days, and bonfires and parties were quite normal, even for the end of November, when the fresh of spring still hung in the air.

It was the shadow that got close enough to catch her eye that made her turn her head and her heart flipped. Before she knew it, she was off the rock and sprinting towards him. She didn't think about being rejected by him now, she just flew into his arms, not caring who saw and what he thought. His lips hungrily found hers and she wrapped her arms around his neck, tears of relief wetting the hair that fell around his ears. She wanted to cry to him to never leave again, but she stopped short of that, knowing that he owed her nothing, that he had to choose where he wanted and needed to be, and when.

When she let go of him, he held her at arm's length and surveyed her. 'New hair? New clothes?'

Mary reddened and cleared her throat. 'These old things?' she said teasingly, with a little sway of her hips.

'And a new attitude … What have you done with my girl?'

'She's here, she's all here,' she said and pulled him close, resting her head on his chest.

'Well, does she have a place for me to stay?' he asked into her hair and she nodded. 'For the summer?'

She jerked herself away from him and stared into his smiling eyes. 'The whole summer?'

'The whole summer,' he repeated.

'What about work?'

'I'm making it my base. I've been doing a little organising and it took some convincing my father, but yes, the whole summer.'

Mary's heart soared and as she held him again, she let the tears roll freely down her face.

CHAPTER 25

It was hard to keep it a secret, but when Lucille left for Melbourne, at the end of December, to settle into Melbourne life, it became a little easier. Lucille was not easily fooled and she questioned her mother about Lawrence often.

'What is going on with you two?' she asked when Mary and Lawrence came up the path. She had been sitting on the armchair and looked at them with such scrutiny that Mary blushed. It occurred to her that this was an abrupt reversal of roles. Lawrence had gone inside the house and Mary had sat in the chair beside her daughter.

'Nothing is going on, young lady,' she scolded. 'And it's not good manners to suggest otherwise.'

'I'm not dumb, Mum,' said Lucille. 'I don't mind, you know. We love Lawrence.'

'Well that's good. I'm glad about that, but there is nothing going on. We are good friends and sometimes it's nice to have friends of the opposite sex.'

'Right,' said Lucille sarcastically. 'Just be careful.'

Lucille looked sad and Mary wanted so badly to confide in her daughter, but the time wasn't right. It was so new, it could crash down on her and on all of them. Maybe in time …

Although Mary detested lying to her daughter, she would rather that than get everyone's hopes up and it all going to hell, which she knew it probably would. Marina didn't seem to notice anything, she was just more infatuated with Lawrence than ever and again, Mary saw her come out of her shell. In those times, she resented Gary for dying and leaving Marina fatherless. But she did worry for Marina. What would happen when Lawrence had to leave again? And as much as she didn't want Marina to rely on Lawrence as a father figure, she enjoyed seeing her daughter with a smile on her face.

Sophie, for her part, didn't need to be told anything; she already seemed to know, and at the beginning, gave Mary knowing smiles and cheeky nudges when Lawrence entered the room.

'So, when are you going to make it public?' said Sophie one afternoon, when they had gone grocery shopping.

'What are you talking about?' Mary was not surprised Sophie had mentioned it. It had been a week since Lucille had left, and she was more surprised that Sophie hadn't mentioned it earlier.

'Come now,' she said. 'I'm a fool for many things, but I have eyes. He looks like he wants to eat you every time he looks at you, and you look like you want to be his tasty snack.' Mary laughed. Sophie always had a way with words. 'I also see you both sneak off into the evening by yourselves. Every evening.'

'Not every evening ...'

'Aha! So some evenings.'

Mary flushed at her naivete. But again, if there was anyone she could trust, it was Sophie. 'Okay, but I don't want to make it public.'

'Who are you hiding it from?'

'Well, mainly the girls …'

'Lucille is not an idiot,' sniffed Sophie. 'Neither am I. Maybe you can fool the little old couple or our sad little friend, Moira, but your daughters …'

'Marina?' Mary was taken aback.

'I don't know, but she's getting quite attached to him.' Sophie's eyes creased in concern.

'I know,' said Mary, troubled.

'Just be careful,' said Sophie.

'Okay.' Mary put her hand on her hip. 'First you tell me to go for it, now be careful?'

'I thought he would be a fling, something to get your mind off your husband …'

'And now?'

'Well, it seems to be going on, so it looks like it's getting serious. What do you know of him?'

Mary was indignant. 'I know what I need to know,' she replied.

'Don't get curly with me,' said Sophie. 'I'm just worried for you.'

'I know. But I also know that I haven't felt anything like this, not for … And I feel like a new person, a different person, someone who is worthy of love again.'

'You see yourself now,' said Sophie nodding. 'But before

everybody else saw it, except you. He is bringing out the best in you. But you've always been the best to us.'

'No, you're the best,' said Mary, hugging her friend. 'You are the best friend I've ever had,' she said.

'Better than Virginia?' Mary pulled a face and Sophie laughed. 'Yes, you're growing up, aren't you?'

'Keep it to yourself for now?'

'Of course I will, but when I'm gone, you will not have anyone to cover for you.'

'You're leaving?'

'At the end of January. For four months, back to Sydney. A movie, a mother part, but it's something I am suited for.' She screwed up her face. 'I have to accept that I'm not going to get the sexy young lady parts anymore.' She looked Mary up and down. 'You'd be quite suited to that though.'

Mary punched her friend in the arm playfully. The fact was that Mary had been feeling differently lately. Whereas before, she put all her energy into the house and her daughters, she now took a moment every day to throw on a splash of makeup and even took time choosing what she would wear. It came back easily now, and she wondered whether she should be making such an effort for a man. But she knew it was about who she was. Lawrence had fallen in love with her when she wore baggy dresses and her hair hung limply. Now she wanted to be the woman she used to be, the one who took care of herself, the one she gave up when Gary died.

CHAPTER 26

'What do you want in life, Mary?' asked Lawrence one hot summer evening when she sat beside the rock, facing the ocean, his arms wrapped around her from behind.

Mary nestled her head in the crook of his arm. 'Mmm. I want this right now.' She felt his nose nudge her hair and leaned into him.

'Me too,' he replied and she felt him sit up.

She turned around to face him, crossing her legs. 'What is it, Lawrence?'

'A future.'

Mary felt a little niggle in her chest. 'What about the future?'

'What do you want?'

'I have everything I want,' she said, trying to banish the image of Gary that floated through her mind.

'Does that include me?'

'Do we have to talk about this now?'

'We don't.' He lowered his eyes.

171

'What's bothering you?'

'I …' He looked up at the clear sky and Mary followed his gaze. 'It's beautiful here. How could I have not known about this kind of beauty?'

Mary looked back at him and his eyes were set intently on hers now. 'It is lovely here.'

'You know that's not what I meant. I've never, in my whole life, felt this,' he said. 'Not with anyone.'

Again Mary thought of Gary. She had. She leaned her head forward onto his. 'This, whatever this is, is beauty,' she said.

'Whatever this is?' He leaned back and narrowed his eyes. 'What is this, Mary?'

Mary got to her feet. This was not the conversation she wanted to have. It was too soon. They had been enjoying each other, loving each other with their bodies, but her heart was still hers and still also belonged to someone else and was at risk of being torn apart by him. 'Can we just enjoy whatever this is?'

He raised himself off the sand and turned her around to face him. 'Is it because of your husband?' Mary felt herself stiffen. 'Or is it because you still have a thing about how old I am?'

How could she tell him it was both? How could she tell him that as much as it shouldn't, his age mattered. She was now in her forties, and he was barely in his thirties. Time would hamper what they now felt about each other. Soon he would tire of her age, of everything that went with it, and who knows how much she would have invested by the time he realised that? She hadn't loved anyone like she'd loved her husband and she still hadn't gotten over the blow of his death all those years ago. She couldn't deal with losing someone else she cared about. Besides, she had responsibilities that he didn't. It had taken so much energy to make a normal, stable life for her children and she couldn't think about what it would take to rebuild that life were it to go sour.

And Gary? How could she ever tell him that he would always come second to the ghost of her husband? The very realisation hit her strongly and she put her head in her hands, to try to stop the sob that erupted from her.

Lawrence pulled her into his arms. 'I'm sorry,' he whispered into her hair. 'It's me. I want too much from you and I know it's too soon.' She clung to him, knowing it was where she wanted to be and still not certain if it was really that simple.

In the past year, she had begun to find out who she was, and it wasn't just a mother and a keeper of a boarding house. She was a woman, who had needs and wants, and she enjoyed rediscovering herself. When Lawrence was not at Jesse's Boarding, she hummed while she worked, looked forward to the morning when she got up a little earlier to spend a few minutes in front of the bathroom mirror, brushing her hair, and putting on a little makeup even if there was no one to notice. But they did notice, and Mary would blush when Mrs Davis would nod and give her a wink of approval. She enjoyed selecting an outfit for her day, not just picking up the first clean thing from her wardrobe.

It wasn't just her appearance that she took care of now. Mary had begun to play the piano again. Since that evening when she had first put her fingers on the keys, she felt a pull to it, an urge that she could barely resist. Then one afternoon, when the Davises were out of the house and Marina was at school, she sat at the stool, the indent fitting her bottom perfectly. She placed her foot on the pedal and pushed down on a key. She kept going, feeling a buzz, nothing like she felt with anything else, and let herself be taken into the world she went into. It was in serious need of tuning but Mary didn't care. She closed her eyes, and when she missed a note, she smiled to herself and didn't stop. She had lost track of time and didn't want to stop, not knowing when she would have the guts to do it again. She wasn't sure how long she had been playing when she finally lifted her hands from the piano and breathed, a soft sigh of pleasure. A shout of claps lurched her backwards and she turned around to see the Davises standing behind her, Mrs Davis beaming in pleasure, a tear running down the side of her face.

'I ... I didn't know anyone was here,' Mary muttered, her heart still thumping from the indulgence of what she had just done.

'My dear Mary,' Mrs Davis said. 'You are still the most beautiful player I ever heard.'

'A bit rusty, Mrs Davis,' said Mary, shyly.

'No, no! That was beautiful to hear.' She came to Mary and placed herself on the corner of the stool. She put her arm around her, resting her head on Mary's shoulder. 'Tell me you will go on. Tell me that I will listen to this again.'

Mary cleared her throat in embarrassment. 'Well, you can certainly play, Mrs Davis. I've never asked you not to.'

Mrs Davis lifted her head and took Mary by the shoulders. 'But I haven't heard anything like this in, oh gosh, how long has it been? Tell me you will continue.'

Mary was surprised when she found herself nodding. She knew she would have to; she had opened this Pandora's box and she couldn't go back. 'I don't know what the time is,' she said, smiling. 'But I think I'm going to have time for one more. Your choice, Mrs Davis.'

'You know what I want,' said Mrs Davis and Mary turned back to the piano, closed her eyes and waltzed into the world of Beethoven.

CHAPTER 27

Sophie said goodbye in January and Mary missed her friend. She popped into the boarding house several times but for very short stays, as the movie she made became a hit and she was busier than ever. Mary missed her confidante, the one who always had her back. But the ever present Davises remained, as did Moira and Lawrence, who had accepted that his room was now his own.

In the summer of '75, Marina declared she was done with studying. She had begun her final year of school and came back at the end of the day, determination written all over her face. Mary sighed inwardly, wondering what was coming, when Marina threw her bag into the corner of the kitchen and sat down at the table, her eyes set on her mother's.

'I'm not going back,' she said.

Mary took a seat and placed her palms on the table, trying to maintain her usual calm but wondering how to deal with this new development. After a couple of minutes of silence, Marina's eyes still boring into hers, Mary took a breath. 'This will be your final year. Just one more. After that you can do whatever you want to do. I've never pushed you in any direction.' She now wished she had and she also wished Lawrence were here. He could probably have dealt with this a little better; he was more removed from the situation and Marina worshipped the ground he walked on.

'I'm ready to work now. I have no great dreams of being anything in particular …'

'But that's what your final year is for. It's to help you figure it out. You could be anything you want to be. You have a good brain and you don't want to waste that.'

'No, I want to work. I want to get a job.'

'To get a good job, you need a good education.'

'You have a job.'

'I run a boarding house. I want more for you.'

'I can work at Looties.' Mary tried not to cringe— Looties was a two-dollar shop in the centre of town and for a summer or part-time job, it would be a wonderful bit of work experience, but to think about Marina working there full time … Mary knew how easily the money she made would prevent her from looking for something else or going back to study.

Mary spent the evening begging and pleading and threatening but she knew that Marina would not budge. Her daughter had shown in the past few years how very stubborn she could be. Again she wished Lawrence were here but Lawrence wouldn't be coming down until the weekend and it wasn't right that she had to rely on him to try to fix her problems as a mother. She hoped that Marina would see reason and change her mind.

When Lucille called as she usually did on Friday evening, she tried to talk to Marina as well but that didn't work and by that time, Marina had already secured a position at Looties. Mary just hoped that she would come to her senses at some point, but no, Marina went to work every day and came back late into the evening. Mary barely saw her anymore and she only showed up for dinner when Lawrence was staying at the house, hanging on every word he said.

Summer slowly eased into a cool autumn again and Mary continued her routine, caring for the boarding house, working on her sewing for the new season, and her financial burden lifted slightly. Lucille came to stay on her term and semester breaks and they would spend the days talking about Lucille's studies which she was loving.

'I'm too early into it to be doing any sort of psychology, but even the nursing is so good. My feet hurt though,' she said. 'And I have to wear these dumpy shoes all day.'

Mary smiled at that. She missed Lucille and pampered her when she visited. Lucille tried to spend time with Marina but her sister, on the verge of eighteen and working full time, had her own life with her own friends that Mary didn't know anything about. She did make an effort to stay for dinner when Lucille was in town, but always kept her eyes on the clock and headed out just after nine.

'Where are you going?' asked Lucille, who was sitting in the lounge ready for a game of gin.

'Out with friends,' said Marina.

'Who?'

'No one you know,' replied Marina and hurried out of the room before the interrogation began.

Lucille looked at Mary in question and Mary shrugged with resignation. 'She does this almost every evening.'

'Mum, she is going out at this time of night? What time does she get home?'

'After twelve, later sometimes.' Mary had been through this with Marina, who threatened to leave the house if she didn't leave her alone.

'Why are you letting this happen?'

'I don't know what to do anymore,' said Mary, tears already escaping her eyes. 'I've tried everything.' She wrung her hands in frustration. 'She won't even listen to Lawrence now. She just does whatever she wants and honestly, I'm powerless to stop it.'

'But you have to. Or else kick her out!'

'I can't do that. I'd rather her be a brat and do whatever and have a place to come home to with people who love her. If I make her leave, she will and then I will have more to worry about.'

'I'm so sorry, Mum,' said Lucille, taking a seat next to Mary and putting her arms around her. 'What about these so-called friends of hers?'

Mary told Lucille about the girl who Marina met at the front of the house, the red-haired girl with some very daring outfits, who didn't even have the decency to acknowledge Mary when she was at the door. Yes, Mary worried terribly about her younger daughter and Lucille had even tried to talk to her, to no avail.

****

The tinkle of the phone was insistent and Mary was roused from her sleep. She looked at the clock which showed 11.35 p.m. and rushed into the reception.

'Mum!' The voice on the other end was breathless.

'Marina?' Mary felt a cold shiver down her back.

'Is Lawrence there?'

'Yes,' replied Mary. Lawrence and Mary had returned from their walk more than an hour ago and he had returned to his room, but a movement made her turn around. He was standing at the door, his hair dishevelled, shirtless and a worried look on his face. 'He's here.'

'Can he come and get me?'

'From where? I can get you.'

'No, not you. I need Lawrence.'

'What's wrong?'

'Can you put him on?'

Lawrence was already putting his hand out for the phone. 'Yes? Okay, where?' He paused and motioned for Mary, who was gesturing wildly, to calm down. 'Are you safe for now?' He paused again. 'Give me ten minutes. Stay where you are.'

'What, what is it?' Mary almost screamed when he hung up.

'She's fine. A problem,' he said as he strode to his room. Mary followed, panic rising in her. 'I'm going to pick her up.'

'I'm coming with you,' said Mary.

'I think it's best you don't,' said Lawrence as he threw on a t-shirt.

'She's my daughter!'

'And she needs me right now,' said Lawrence and shoved on his shoes. He stood up and his face softened when he saw the terror in Mary's eyes. 'She is okay. A bit of a problem with a boy.'

Mary's eyes widened. 'Did he ...'

'I think she's tougher than you know.' He kissed her forehead. 'I won't be long.'

Mary watched him drive away and sat on the porch, biting her fingernails. She prayed her daughter was all right. What could have happened to her? Why would she be asking for Lawrence? She rocked back and forth, her heart in her mouth, looking at her watch every few seconds. Less than half an hour later, she heard Lawrence's car drive into the carpark and it took every inch of her to remain on the porch and not run to them. Marina looked sheepishly at her mother as she came into view, kissed her cheek and scurried into the house. Lawrence pulled up a chair and sat by Mary.

'What happened?' she asked when she saw Lawrence's jaw tighten.

'Marina shouldn't be working there,' he said.

'What? At the store?'

'She was not working at the store,' he replied.

'Where was she working?' Mary didn't understand what

181

he was saying.

'At Lazy Al's.'

Mary brought her hand to her mouth. Everyone knew what Lazy Al's was. A strip club on the other side of town, the sleazy part that no one in Righteous Creek talked about, but everyone knew about. 'What?!'

'She's been working there for the last two months apparently.'

'How did I not know?'

'She went out when you thought she'd gone to bed.'

Suddenly it made sense. Marina had taken many days off lately as she slept in and Mary wondered how her manager at the store kept her on with that kind of attendance. Mary had never asked about her pay or what she did with it and Marina had never needed money from her, so she figured she was okay. She always seemed to have it, even buying new clothes in the last few weeks and Mary even commented on her tasteful choices. How could she not see what was happening? She never visited the store because she didn't want Marina to think she was checking up on her and she wanted to leave her to her own devices, treat her like the adult she thought she was. But this!

'I neglected her,' she said almost to herself.

'You didn't do anything.' Lawrence put his hand on Mary's that were shivering in a ball. She withdrew it and looked at Lawrence.

'That's right, I didn't,' replied Mary. 'I should have done something. I should have known something.'

'This is not your fault.'

'What happened tonight?'

'One of the patrons got frisky. Followed her out when she went for a smoke ...'

'She smokes too?' How could she have not known that either? Smelled it on her? On her clothes?

'Well, anyway. He got a little too ... handsy.'

'Where was everyone else?'

'Inside, I guess. She managed to get inside too, but he was waiting for her. But she was scared. It wasn't the first time ...'

'What did you do?'

Lawrence looked at his hands and Mary followed his gaze. His knuckles were red and the back of his hands were grazed. She looked at his face and noticed a bump on his cheekbone.

'What did you do?' she repeated, fear coursing through her body.

'I dealt with it.'

'Right,' she said and then burst into tears. Lawrence pulled her to him and she sobbed into his shirt.

'It's my fault. I was so wrapped up in everything, in you, I just thought, I just hoped ...'

'It's not your fault, but we do have to figure out what to do about Marina. She's lost. She needs to find herself or else it will get worse.'

****

'You will work at the boarding house for me,' said Mary the next morning, when Marina, still in her pyjamas, strolled into the kitchen at eleven in the morning rubbing her eyes and yawning. It was time for an ultimatum, time to set things straight, and if Marina didn't want to accept her offer, Mary was going to turn her out. It would break her heart to do that to her daughter, but she had to get tough. Nothing else was working and after last night's revelation, she just didn't know what would happen with her child. Mary fixed her gaze on Marina.

'No. I have a job.' Marina's defiant eyes stared back into hers.

'Well, either that, or you're out on your own. If you continue to work at that place, you will have enough money to pay for a place of your own anyway.'

'You can't tell me what to do,' she said without emotion.

Mary tried not to waver. She could tell Marina was considering the options. 'As long as you live here, yes, I can. If you choose to continue to do what you've been doing, you're quite welcome to leave. You're nearly an adult now.'

Marina turned her head towards the window, at the shadow of Lawrence, who was leaning on the fence out on the porch. She strode out the door and Mary, peering through the window, saw her striding to the edge of the water. Her hands were folded and she kicked at the sand. She saw Lawrence follow and prayed he would talk some sense into her.

When they came back in, Marina shrugged at Mary and left the room. Lawrence nodded; he had convinced her. Mary let out the breath that she'd been holding and sat down at the table.

'Maybe we should stop seeing each other for a while,' said Mary when they went for a stroll in the evening.

'If you wish,' Lawrence replied, his eyes on the path ahead.

Mary shivered. She didn't expect him to succumb so easily. He was the only thing that gave her joy. The last year or so had been tough with Lucille leaving, Marina's antics, and Sophie had been away so often, she hadn't anyone to talk to. Lawrence had been the one she leaned on and now she thought, maybe a little too much. But she loved him. And even though he hadn't said it, they both knew he felt the same. It was in the things he did, the way he looked at her, the time they spent together. How could he not?

'If that's what you want,' he said softly.

She stopped and looked at him. 'What do you want?'

'You know what I want. But I also know you are uneasy about us. You haven't told anyone about us being together.'

'Isn't it too soon?'

He smirked. 'Do you think, after all this time, it's too soon?'

Mary was flustered. This wasn't where the conversation was meant to go. She was worried about Marina and was looking for some sort of solution. 'I don't know. I don't know.'

'I know it's Marina we have to think about,' he said, reading her thoughts.

'Yes, it's Marina, but …'

He took her face in his hands. 'Are you still not sure about me? About how I feel for you?'

'You've never said it.'

'I love you, Mary. From the moment I met you.'

She couldn't say it back even though she felt it, more deeply than she wished she did. She took his hands from her face and turned away. 'There's just …'

'I know. You've been caught up on the age thing …'

'It's not that,' she cried, knowing that part of it was just that. But she also had so many other responsibilities. There was Marina now and she still clearly needed her.

'It's okay. I'll be ready when you are. I'm not going anywhere.'

CHAPTER 28

Mary hung up the phone and sighed. Perhaps it was good timing. Lawrence was not at home and Marina had been brooding since that night two weeks ago. Maybe a trip away from here would help her daughter. And her. A new scene, somewhere that would give her a new lease on life, perspective from afar.

Marina had not wanted to leave the house and spent every day in her room, only leaving it when Lawrence arrived to spend the weekend, and Mary found herself resenting both of them, Lawrence for being there for her daughter, and Marina, for not allowing her in. She still felt a sense of relief that at least Marina saw him as someone she could trust and that was better than no one.

'Does she talk to you about how she's feeling?' Mary was loathe to ask Lawrence about her own daughter but she was beyond desperation.

'She seems lonely, but she doesn't talk to me about anything in particular.'

'Do you think she'll grow out of it?'

'I don't know, Mary. We just have to be there for her, I guess.' He took her hands in his. 'Both of us,' he said so earnestly, Mary felt her heart fill with hope. Maybe it was time. For them to be together, to show a united front as a couple. For Marina to understand that Lawrence was part of her family too.

Mary knocked on Marina's door and as usual got no answer. She opened it and found Marina on her lounge chair, drawing. At least that was something she was interested in. She had barely helped with the running of Jesse's Boarding and never took the initiative, only did anything around the place when Mary asked her to. Marina turned her head to Mary and gave her a crooked smile. Encouraged, Mary moved forward and sat on the edge of her bed.

'What do you think about going with me to Perth for a while?'

Marina made a face. 'Perth?'

'Just for a little while.'

'What's in Perth?'

'Well, your grandparents for one.'

'Have I met them?'

'Sure, when you were little. They moved up when you were about, let's see, two, maybe three?'

'I don't remember. Why haven't we seen them in all this time?'

'Well, that's a long story, but maybe it's time to meet them, properly this time.'

Marina narrowed her eyes. 'Why now?'

Mary sighed. 'My father is dying.'

'Oh.' Marina left her mouth in an O.

'And my mother needs me.'

'I'm sorry,' Marina managed. 'Why don't you ever talk about them?'

'I have sometimes,' Mary said defensively. 'What do you want to know?'

'Anything really.'

'Let's see ...' Mary tried to think of something nice to say about her parents, something that would make them somewhat enticing to Marina, but she couldn't think of anything.

'Do I have to go?' Marina frowned.

Mary thought about her mother, looking at her daughter with disdain, the things she would say to her. 'No, you don't. But I have to go.'

'Who's going to take care of the place when you're gone?' Marina's eyes were beginning to light up.

'I'll have to keep it closed while I'm away. The Davises and Moira can manage to take care of themselves for a while.' Mary was already calculating the losses from the bookings that had been made for the next month that would have to be cancelled but she could manage with the savings she had put away.

Marina almost jumped out of her chair. 'I can take care of the place when you're gone. I can run things here so you won't have to shut it down. I know everything you do. And Lawrence can help.'

Mary was taken aback and a little lost for words. Marina

had shown no interest in the place before this. 'Um...' Mary began.

'Please, Mum,' said Marina. 'I've been good. I'll show you I can be responsible. The Davises are here too, and Moira, and they can help out if I need them.'

'But running things is different to helping out, Marina.'

'I know what you do. You can leave a list. You can call every day if you want. If something goes wrong, I'll call you back, or I'll shut the house.' Mary was silent for a moment, considering this option, and watched Marina's face, so animated with pleasure, something she hadn't seen in a very long time. Maybe this was what Marina needed. To be treated like an adult, which she would be very soon, to be given responsibilities, not just chores. 'And if worse comes to worst, I'll call Lu. She's only in the city.'

'Let me think about it,' said Mary and was surprised when Marina thew herself onto her, launching her back onto her bed. She hadn't been hugged by her daughter in she couldn't remember how long. She held her tight, knowing she was going to do it already and it was the right thing to do.

****

Lawrence drove her to the train station on a Friday afternoon and Mary was silent for most of the way, her hands held tight in the folds of her skirt, her mind on whether the instructions she had left with Marina and the Davises were clear. Two weeks, she told herself, that was all. She had paid all the bills for the next month and had given Marina instructions if something came up.

'It will be okay,' Lawrence had said. 'I will stay here most of the time. I'm arranging it so I can make this my permanent base. I was going to do that anyway.' He smiled sheepishly. 'No point in wasting the room you keep reserved for me.' He winked.

'I never ...' Mary began and then laughed. There was no point in hiding the fact that she waited for him to come to stay. 'But I don't want to put any responsibility on you. This is not your doing.'

'I know, but when I'm here, we're a family anyway.'

Mary's heart warmed at those words and she smiled as she thought about them now, her hands relaxing. Lawrence reached out and held on to them, not asking her for any small talk and she appreciated it. She didn't want to talk about leaving the house, leaving her child to manage it, and leaving him. She didn't want to see her parents, not one of them, but she had to go. They had no one else. 'I'll be back in a couple of weeks, hopefully,' she said, trying to convince herself more than she was Lawrence.

'What are you expected to do there?' Lawrence asked as they stood on the platform, waiting for the last call.

'Help out, I guess. Maybe once he's gone ...'

'I'm sorry.'

'Don't be sorry.' Mary wasn't sure if she herself was sorry, she didn't even know who those people were. 'I thought he'd outlive all of us. He was so full of life.' she said bitterly.

'I wish I could go with you,' said Lawrence.

'I wouldn't do that to you,' said Mary with a smirk. 'They didn't have time for me, they certainly will not have any for you.' It was the first time in a long time she felt the pang of neglect and she felt it now, so sudden, so painful. 'Anyway, I think I will probably need to set her up in a nursing home or something. From the way she sounded, I don't think she's too far behind.'

'What if she wants to come to live with you?'

Mary looked at him in horror. She'd never considered that. 'Oh gosh, no!'

'We need to be there for our folks, especially in their old age.'

'You've clearly never met my parents,' she said, trying to keep the resentment from her voice.

The voice of the conductor boomed out on the loudspeaker and Mary picked up her suitcase.

'I'll miss you,' she said.

'You be careful,' he replied. 'Don't go running off with some handsome man.'

She laughed. 'Not when I have one to come back to,' she replied. He kissed her softly and she boarded the train. She took her seat and watched as he disappeared from sight.

CHAPTER 29

The moment she alighted the train, she knew she had made a mistake. A niggling feeling had nudged at her throughout the train ride and she couldn't help but feel this was a trip that would change things, and not for good. She'd spent the last three days riding on the train with thoughts of Lawrence and her daughters running through her mind. She worried they would not cope and thought about turning around more than once. But she wanted to let Marina have some time on her own, and Lawrence, well, she was missing him more than ever. Even though for the most part, she spent the whole week without him, she knew he was not more than a few hours away. But Perth. That seemed like a world away.

She kept reliving the events of their last night. It had begun in the early evening, before dinner, when she had sat at the piano and Lawrence had sat beside her, using his left hand on the keys, while she played with her right. She was teaching him 'Begin The Beguine' and he had picked it up really well.

Since the day she had played so passionately, the sound of the piano was heard often, Mrs Davis and even Moira using it. Mary couldn't help but think of Gary when she heard the sound echo through the house, but she didn't feel her gut fall between her legs at the sound as she used to. Now she beamed in happiness and let her feet move to the sound. Even Marina had wanted to try it and she'd tried to teach her, but Marina, Mary could see, wasn't that interested and tired of it quickly. Mrs Davis played often now, taking the chance to have a new student in the form of Moira, who was eager to learn.

When Lawrence had come to stay on that weekend, she knew she had to try to break the curse and she led him to the piano. His eyes had widened in surprise but he sat beside her on the stool and she ran her fingers along the length of the piano, letting herself feel its power without Gary beside her. And she played, glorious melodies that reverberated through the air. When she played the last note of 'La Vie En Rose', she breathed deeply and smiled, her eyes still closed. She did it. With Lawrence beside her, not Gary, but Lawrence. She turned to him, her skin on fire, and watched as he raised his dropped jaw.

'What ...' he stuttered.

'Did I tell you I used to play the piano?' she said, raising her eyebrows.

'No. You didn't. What did I just hear?'

'I used to play. I am playing again,' she said simply. 'Want to try?' She narrowed her eyes. 'Or do you also have some secret that I don't know about?'

He laughed. 'There's no way I'm touching that thing after what I just heard.' He looked at the piano and poked at it gingerly with his forefinger.

'Want to hear a bit more?' she asked, her hands itching to touch those keys again.

'Yes, always,' he said and looked around before he planted a quick kiss on her cheek.

And they had played together each time he came to stay, Mary enjoying the feeling it gave her and enjoying teaching Lawrence different songs. On occasion, a number of the guests would cram into the little hallway, listening and taking turns, and Mary had even gotten a tuner to be able to play in all the glorious splendour of the instrument.

****

Mary's eyes welled as she sat in the darkness of her compartment, watching dabs of light go past through the window as the train churned onto its path, her path now. She had never not wanted to do anything more in her life. Everything she loved remained behind and all that lay ahead was misery. She turned her thoughts back to Lawrence and managed a slight smile, trying to keep the memory of him with her, keeping alive the last night of being together.

Mary and Lawrence, after dinner and the cleaning had been done, were about to take their regular evening walk and they both smiled at each other with a mixture of relief and sadness. At least they had this evening to themselves. They had just rounded the corner and Lawrence's hand reached for hers as it usually did when they were out of sight of the boarding house.

'Wait, I'm coming with you,' they heard behind them and turned to see Marina bouncing towards them. Lawrence's hand jerked back to himself, and Mary shuddered at the thought that Marina could have seen them as more than friends. So far, they had kept it to themselves, managing to keep their affection away from the eyes of everyone at the house, even though the sly remarks of the Davises made Mary realise that they hadn't really fooled everyone. Except Marina, who seemed so caught up in herself that Mary was relieved she was not that interested in the goings-on around her. Where Marina was concerned, Mary was just happy her daughter was returning to the person she used to be before she changed. She still didn't know what, if anything, instigated that change and was not sure she would ever find out. She was just happy her child seemed to be herself again and figured it had to be the fact that she was being given control of the house and the fact that Lawrence was staying for the duration of Mary's absence. She just hoped she wouldn't give him too much trouble.

Marina tucked herself between them as they walked in the cool air, regretful glances behind Marina's back the only communication they had. Marina had chattered away about how she was going to do the work for the house, and how she was looking forward to running the place. Mary had a sudden sense of foreboding, and wondered yet again whether she was doing the right thing and reassuring herself that it would be just for a couple of weeks.

When they reached the house, Mary and Lawrence lingered, waiting for Marina to go to her room but she filled herself a glass of water and sat at the dining table and Lawrence, with a sorry nod of his head, bade them both goodnight.

'I'm going to bed too,' said Mary and Marina frowned. 'Do you want me to stay with you for a bit?' Marina shrugged and Mary sat opposite her, surveying her child, trying to figure what was going on in her mind. After a while, Marina looked up at her mother and Mary could tell she'd already changed her mind about confiding in her. 'Do you want to discuss something?'

'No,' said Marina.

'Are you worried about running this place?'

Marina shook her head slowly. 'No. I think I will be okay.'

'You can talk to me, you know.'

Marina nodded again and Mary knew she was not going to open up. 'I may go to bed too,' said Marina as she stood. 'I'll be fine, Mum,' she said and kissed the top of her mother's head. Mary grabbed her arm and clung to it, Marina resting her head on the top of her mother's.

'Goodnight, Marina,' Mary said. 'I love you.'

'Love you too,' said Marina and as her daughter walked out of the room, Mary stared at her back in stunned silence. She hadn't heard that from her child in a very long time. She put Marina's glass in the sink and looked out into the darkness. She would miss this, just watching the beach, even the eerie feel it had to it now, when she was in Perth. She went to bed.

After two hours of tossing and turning and checking the clock on the nightstand, Mary got out of bed and went into the kitchen. She poured herself a glass of water and stared again into the night. She knew she was not going to sleep tonight and wished Lawrence were out here with her. She hated that they didn't have the chance to say a proper goodbye, that the last bit of time they had was taken. She thought about him constantly, a tingle in her body when she did, waiting to be sated.

She felt guilty at the thought. It was her daughter that had interrupted their plans and her children always came first. But the selfish part of Mary, the one she allowed to be part of her now, cried out. She wanted to spend time with Lawrence. Sure, he would be driving her to the station the next day, but she knew she wouldn't have time with him, just to be. As it was, she was already so nervous about this trip.

'Couldn't sleep either?' Mary spun around to see Lawrence, his hair mussed, coming through the kitchen door. 'No, I guess not.' Even though he wore a black t-shirt, Mary could see his skin cling to it, and even in the mood she was in, her body stirred. She swallowed as he approached, and she peered behind him. She knew she didn't need to. No one in their right mind was awake at this hour, but she still worried.

He moved towards her and removed a strand of hair from her forehead. 'Stay with me tonight,' he whispered, his mouth so close to her ear, she could feel the warmth of his breath. She stiffened for a second and then took his hand and nodded.

She was in his arms only for a few short hours but Mary knew she belonged there, near him, feeling his skin pressed tight to hers. She decided right then that it was time. This thing they had was not going to go away, Lawrence was not going away, and it was time for them to have their love out in the open, his age be damned. She had yet to tell him how she really felt, but she knew she didn't need to. He knew.

****

She shifted in her little seat, wishing she could have afforded a berth, but she calculated she was more than halfway to Perth by now. She fell in and out of sleep and walked the aisles along with other people who also needed to stretch their legs, trying to ignore the sick feeling in her belly, and remembered how she had motion sickness when she was just five when her parents had taken her on a trip to Sydney to visit her grandmother. She had vomited all over the back seat and was swiftly yanked out of the car after her father had pulled over. Her mother cussed at her and roughly wiped away the mess on her dress. She was put into a shirt, a paper bag promptly placed on her chest.

She tried now not to think about her parents and the first and last time she visited them here. More than fifteen years ago, just her and the children. She had lasted three days and gone right home after her parents showed not just disinterest in her arrival, but distaste in her children. She knew she wouldn't be taking them back. If they had any interest in her life, they were welcome to come to see her. She thought of the conversation, if that's what one would call it, with her mother on the phone. She had almost dropped the phone when she heard her mother's voice say her name tentatively.

'Mother?' Mary had questioned once she recovered.

'Yes, it's Mother,' said the voice. 'Are you very busy?'

Mary was not sure where the conversation was headed. 'Um ...'

'I need you to come down to Perth for a while.'

'Okay ...' Mary said slowly.

'If you feel like it.' The voice dripped with derision.

'Is everything okay?'

'Well if you wrote once in a while, maybe you would know your father is not well.'

Mary's heart lurched. 'I can be there in a few days,' she said.

'Good. He hasn't got long.'

Despite herself, Mary felt her eyes well. 'I'll be there.'

'Same address as before. We'll see you soon.'

She had hung up the phone and rested on the chair at the counter. She couldn't make head nor tail of that conversation. She hadn't seen or spoken to her parents in more than a decade and a half and suddenly this? Of course she had thought about them, wanted to visit, to call, but they didn't have a phone at the time so there was no way to contact them. But she knew they were not interested in her and the last time she contacted them was when Gary had died when she'd sent a letter informing them of his death. She'd heard nothing in return, which was when she decided that she had had enough of trying to be loved by them.

Now this.

It was past five thirty in the evening when the train rolled to a stop with a fuss, all noise and smoke, and Mary held her mouth, trying to quell the sickness that was coming up through her throat. She stood on the platform and considered what to do now. She couldn't turn back. Maybe they had changed. She doubted it very much from the conversation with her mother on the phone, the same stilted voice, the same disdain.

The first thing she did was locate a phone booth and dial the boarding house.

'Jesse's Boarding, how may I help you?' came the chirpy voice of Marina, and Mary couldn't believe how different her daughter sounded.

'Hi, darling,' said Mary, a lump in her throat.

'Mum! Where are you? Are you there yet?'

'I've just arrived. How's everything there?'

'Well, this family came yesterday and they are going to extend their stay for a week. I've already done the shopping for the week. Lawrence took me. I'm making pancakes for breakfast tomorrow. This is fun.'

Mary smiled at the enthusiasm in her daughter's voice. 'Good, good. Are you coping? Everything okay?'

'Stop worrying. Everything is fine. Lawrence will come up tomorrow again, so he said he'd help out.'

At the mention of Lawrence Mary felt a stab in her heart. She missed him so much already and he had barely left her mind since she had left him at the station. 'Good. Okay. I'm still at the station and I smell. I need to shower and change. I'll call you tomorrow.'

'Okay, and try to have fun, Mum. Maybe find yourself a man there.'

Mary almost dropped the phone with that comment. 'Marina!'

'Just have a good time, Mum. Be safe.' Marina laughed.

Mary hung up the phone and hailed a taxi. They would be okay, she could hear it in her daughter's voice, but she still had a tough road ahead dealing with her parents. As she sat in the backseat of the taxi trying to ignore the churning of her stomach which was aided by the inane questions of the driver, she found her palms were clammy and rubbed them over her skirt. She suddenly realised she hadn't prepared for meeting them, had purposely tried not to think about it in the week since she had spoken to her mother.

They had left Righteous Creek just before she married Gary, not even waiting for her wedding, which in all fairness to them, had been a pretty hasty affair. And in their defence they had already planned to leave before Gary asked for her hand. They hadn't even bothered to show up for the wedding, not even a call. And when she had written to let them know of the birth of their grandchildren, they sent a curt congratulatory card.

Now she wondered what awaited her. Why had her mother called her? And why was she going? The drive to their house was a long one and although it gave Mary a chance to gather her thoughts, by the time the taxi pulled up to the kerb, she was a nervous wreck.

'Fourteen dollars and twenty-two cents,' said the driver, and Mary shuffled through her wallet, giving him the amount with a tip.

'Thanks,' she said and held the door handle for a moment too long.

'You okay, Mrs?'

'Yep, I think so.'

'Do you need help with your luggage?'

'No,' said Mary, swallowing. 'I'm okay.'

The driver nevertheless got out to retrieve her suitcase from the boot and stood waiting for her to exit the cabin. When she finally got the courage to open the car door, the driver was already hauling her case to the front door. Mary wanted to call for him to stop, to take her back to the station, but she saw the front light turn on. She raised her chin and walked swiftly to the door, giving the driver an appreciative nod as he walked back to the car.

CHAPTER 30

'Hello, Mother,' said Mary to the old woman who stood
with a walking stick at the door. If Mary hadn't been so nervous,
she would have dropped her jaw in shock at the look of this
woman, whose creased eyes and bent back were a far cry from
the vivacious, proud woman of fifteen years ago.

'Come in,' said her mother, her eyes not even on Mary's
for a second, and led her in. 'You know where everything is.'

Mary didn't. It had been a long time since she had been
here, but the smell when she entered reminded her of why she
never wanted to return. The perfume, she knew it well and
almost gagged every time the scent floated through her nostrils
when at a shopping centre or wafted behind a guest who arrived
at the boarding house. She felt her stomach turn and held her
mouth. A flash of dizziness hit her and she held the wall to steady
herself.

'This will be your room.' Mary followed her mother into
a small room with a single bed facing a window with bars
covering it. 'I've had dinner already but if you're hungry, there's
a milk bar down the road. They sell hot dogs and pies as well.
There's leftover pot roast in the fridge but I don't suppose you'd
want that.'

Mary was starving and the pot roast sounded good but

the invitation to eat it wasn't terribly inviting. 'Thanks, I may go to the store.'

'When you're settled, come see your father.' Her mother closed the door behind her.

Mary sat on the bed and put her head in her hands. Right now she wanted to talk to Lawrence, to hear his soothing voice tell her it would be okay, that she would be home soon and in his arms. Here she was in the home of her parents, Julia and Samuel, where she should feel comfort, feel safe, but it was the last place on earth she ever felt that and the isolation she felt as a child crept back into her bones. She looked around for a phone but there wasn't one in the room and she supposed they may keep it in the living room. She changed her clothes, desperate for a shower but she didn't want to ask her mother if she could have one. The reception she received didn't surprise her, not at all; in fact, it was what she'd expected, but that little hole in her heart, she realised, still wanted to be filled by parental love.

Two weeks in this place! An idea struck her. Maybe she could stay at a hotel. But no; apart from the fact she couldn't afford to, her mother had asked her to stay with them for a reason. What exactly that was, she didn't know, as Julia clearly had shown no newfound affection for her daughter. She went out of the room and found her mother in the lounge room. She stood tentatively at the door.

'Did you have a good trip?'

Mary nodded. 'Yes,' she replied. 'A long one.'

'That sounds like a complaint.' Her mother didn't look at her but got up and Mary, trying to hold back a retort, followed her to a closed door. Julia knocked and there was no answer, but she opened the door and went in anyway. Mary put her hand to her chest in shock and gasped at the man who lay on the bed, a tube in his nose, his eyes closed. 'Looks different, doesn't he?'

Mary moved closer to the bed and if she had seen this man on the street, she never would have recognised him. The sharp features of her once handsome father were crumpled, his skin was discoloured and his hands, which were placed on the top of the covers, were bent. She felt a tear well and took a deep breath. 'What's the prognosis?'

'None. He will be gone in a week, maybe a few days more. May God have mercy and take him tonight.'

Mary blanched. 'What?'

'Got sent home from the hospital last week.'

'He's only sixty-four.'

'He's lived. By God, he has lived. More than me and I'm sure more than you. No, he is ready to go.' She said it without emotion and Mary realised her mother had been living with this knowledge for a while and her absence of sentiment was acceptance.

Her father moved slightly and Mary wanted to take his hand but she knew it would be the wrong thing to do. Her mother eyed her, almost defying her to. Yes, her mother was the strong one, the one who always won. And now, Mary wished she had fought back; maybe she could at least have been close to one parent. On impulse, she took his hand and stroked it.

'Now you care?' Julia said immediately.

'I'm here, aren't I?' Mary shot back without turning around. She decided enough was enough. She had come all this way, leaving everything she cared about back in Righteous

Creek, and she had become a respectable woman, despite her parents. No, she wasn't going to be the weakling with her mother anymore.

'Better late than never, you think?' Julia had her hands on her hips.

'Why did you call me?' Mary turned to face her mother, curious to know why only now she needed her there.

Her mother looked back at her father and her face softened. 'Because he wanted to see you.'

Mary nodded and her mother left the room with a little sniff, and Mary realised her mother was not a cold-hearted, loveless woman. She just had enough love for one person and she heaped that love on her husband, and him alone. There was none left for the daughter she never wanted. Mary sat on the chair next to the bed and held her father's hand, waiting for him to stir, but even though she stayed for over an hour, her father didn't wake. Mary was more tired than hungry so when she came out of the room and her mother was nowhere to be seen, she headed to bed.

She lay there thinking about Lawrence and Marina and hoped they were coping. She wished she could have called them, just to check in again. She longed to hear Lawrence's voice and imagined him sitting with her, talking, laughing, making love. They found ways to be together, in the car, like teenagers, on the beach like vagrants, in the ocean like fish, and every minute they were not together was a minute she missed him.

Every Friday between four and five in the afternoon he arrived, leaving early on Monday morning, and when he had holidays, for weeks at a time, sometimes, he spent his whole time with her. Yes, she knew she loved him but there was no way she would put him above her children. Lucille and Marina were her life, and she would give her own for them.

Gary floated through her mind now. Would she have given up everything for Gary? Even her children? She loved Gary more than anything and she let herself think about him now. She hadn't in so long, trying to focus on the future, not live in the past, but here, staying with these people, whom he'd rescued her from, she couldn't help but love him, not just for taking her away from them, but for all the love he gave her, warm, true, unconditional love. The first time she had felt that way. She hadn't known how to receive it, kept thinking he would eventually discover out she was unlovable and leave her. She sighed. He did leave eventually.

'A week, maybe a little more,' she said to herself and closed her eyes, hoping at least some sleep would come to her in this strange place.

She left consciousness at close to four a.m. but the sound of movement in the house not long after roused her from her fitful sleep. Her stomach growled and Mary realised she hadn't eaten anything since breakfast the day before. She got out her toiletries and headed to the bathroom, which she had located on her way to her room the night before. It was vacant, so she showered, brushed her teeth and went out into the house to find her mother. She entered the kitchen to find her sitting at the table, her head in her hands.

'Mother?'

Her mother's head snapped up in surprise and she glared at Mary. Then she forced a smile and Mary was a little uneasy. She hadn't seen one that was aimed at her, not in a very long time. 'Do you want breakfast?'

Mary nodded, wondering what was in store. Usually her own kitchen had the aromas of bacon or pancakes or eggs and fresh bread floating about in the morning but she reproached herself for her judgement. Not everybody had to care for any number of guests at a time. 'What's on offer?' She tried to sound light and moved about the kitchen, trying to ignore the smell of that perfume that seemed to be everywhere and was making her nauseous.

'There are cornflakes, your dad's favourite. And Weetbix. Milk is in the fridge.'

Mary was somewhat relieved. She needed something dry to quell the uneasiness in her stomach. 'Would you like some too?' Her mother shook her head and Mary made the breakfast and sat at the table opposite her mother. There was an awkward silence, the only sound breaking it, the food being crunched in Mary's mouth. Her mother stirred and sipped at her tea.

'So what's wrong with Dad?' What Mary really wanted to ask was *Why am I here?* It was clear nothing had changed and she had hoped that maybe after all this time there was some sense of regret, of remorse about the way they had been with her, but it didn't look like it. She felt just as unwanted as always, a stranger in her parents' home.

Her mother shrugged. 'What isn't? Everything is failing now.'

Despite her thoughts, Mary reached out her hand and placed it on her mother's and felt a thud in her heart, waiting for a rebuff. But her mother let it remain and put her other hand on top of hers. It was the slightest gesture but Mary's throat clogged and she felt the urge to cry. She wanted to get up and go over to her mother's side of the table, hug her, tell her how she felt and what she wanted, which was to be loved by them, but she knew that was pushing it. 'Need me to do anything today? Go to the store? Get something?'

Her mother retrieved her hand and stood up abruptly. 'No. Maybe afterwards. I need to go out to call Doctor Little. He was meant to come yesterday.'

'You can't call him from here?' Mary looked around for a phone.

'No phone,' said her mother. 'Can't afford it. Don't need it.'

'But Dad ...' Mary thought it was absurd that they didn't have a telephone. Especially with her father literally on his deathbed.

'We do things the old-fashioned way here. We walk to the phone booth when we need to make a call.'

Mary was sure there had been a phone the last time she was here, but she understood again how her parents didn't have time for anyone but themselves. They lived in their little world and the rest be damned.

The next two weeks were spent in a routine of waking, eating and waiting for Mary's father to wake. She spent the rest of her time cleaning the house, trying to rid it of the scent of Chanel, and found satisfaction in chores, feeling like it was part of her routine at the boarding house. Her mother had fallen down the front steps and had broken her hip, hence the walking stick, and Mary understood why the house was a mess. Her mother made conversation when they ate together, enquired politely about the children, the house, her life, and Mary brushed off the questions with just as polite but brief answers. At least Julia was trying to have a conversation with her, was aware that she existed. But Mary had no illusions about the fate of their

210

relationship and wondered what was going to happen when her father died.

Her parents didn't even own a car, so she trudged a kilometre to the phone booth every couple of days to check in on the boarding house and when she heard the voices of Marina and Lawrence, she wanted to cry, so desperate she was to be back home. Everything seemed to be going well and Marina seemed to be a different person, so mature, so adult and Mary was glad she had entrusted the responsibility of Jesse's Boarding to her. But whenever she went back to her parents' house after an errand, and especially after a phone call home, Mary felt ill, not just mentally but physically. She felt guilty for counting the days until she could return home but she knew what that would mean. And her mother? What was to become of her? She had not talked about what was to happen after her father died and Mary was certainly not going to bring it up. She had no idea what plans her mother had in store for her. Besides she couldn't tell how it would upset her mother and right now there was an uneasy truce that she didn't want to break. She would deal with what happened when it happened.

When her father passed away, without having woken up to see her, Mary was disappointed and regretful that she hadn't had the chance to say goodbye and to tell him that after everything, she still loved him. And she did. She wept for him, for their relationship and for the father he should have been and realised too late. The funeral was a lonely affair with just the nurse who came to check on him twice a week and a couple that clearly had not been in touch for a long time. There were stilted greetings and her mother held her head high, not shedding a tear.

Mary wondered about her mother's absence of emotion until she got up in the middle of the night to have a drink of water. She was feeling nauseous again and the thought of returning home made her stomach churn with yearning. That was when she heard stifled sobs emanating from her mother's bedroom. Mary closed her eyes and leaned against the door, desperate to soothe the woman who had only loved one person. She knew that love well and she felt the tears fall against the door as she thought of Gary and the sobs she had to hide from the world. She knew that nothing and no one, especially not herself, could help her mother. She made her way to the kitchen and tried to think about what awaited her when she got home, and her heart felt lighter. Mary was ready to go back to where she belonged.

And then everything changed.

CHAPTER 31

The words of the doctor announcing triumphantly that she was with child blurred as Mary felt her knees weaken. She felt an arm stop her from hitting the floor and she was being led to a seat. She took the offered glass of water and gulped it down. Her throat was dry and her thoughts were hazy. She was unable to process what was happening. She had gone to the doctor to get some sickness pills to prepare for the train ride back home, whenever that was, but she hoped it would be as soon as possible and she wanted to be prepared.

'Pregnant?' she asked the kindly old man who was on his haunches in front of her, his eyes crinkled in concern.

'Yes, but it would be good if you could take a blood test to be sure.' He hesitated and she saw his eyes flicker to her left hand. 'This is not good news?'

Mary put her head in her hands. What was happening here? Lawrence had been careful, they both had been. How could this have happened? Besides, she was too old to be pregnant. 'What about my age?' She lifted her head in hope.

'How old are you, Mary?'

'Forty-one,' she said dumbly. She knew biology. It had been one of her favourite subjects at school.

213

'That's not too old to bear children. Did you think …'

I'm not stupid, she wanted to yell at him. She just didn't think that there would be a chance, especially when they had been so careful.

'What would you like to do?'

'I have to go,' she said and rushed out of the doctor's office. She didn't need a blood test. She knew what it felt like to be pregnant. She had had three pregnancies. She should have known already. Three pregnancies, two births. The last one was the final straw. Gary never returned from that one. He had been too weak to cope with it, and she had to by herself, while he went … A stab of resentment went through her and the image of Virginia's vindictive, triumphant face popped into her head.

She knew she was letting other thoughts cloud her mind. She couldn't begin to process what this meant. She wandered home on foot, taking more than two hours to reach her parents' home. She was numb, thoughts of her predicament running through her head. She couldn't have this baby! She was too old to do it all again. And Lawrence! He had said many times he didn't want to be a father again either. One too many losses had hurt him too much. She thought at the time that he was saying it because he didn't want her to feel old, that her not wanting any more children wasn't a hindrance to his dreams of being a father again. But he had insisted again and again that he didn't want to have any more children and she knew he didn't. She didn't either so nothing more was thought of it.

But when she held her hand to her stomach in bed that night, she wasn't sure she could give it up. No, this was a life granted to her and one that she was going to protect. She knew it right away. She needn't have Lawrence's permission to keep something that was hers. If he didn't want it, well, she had brought up two children practically on her own anyway. She wasn't sure about how good a job she'd done but living with her mother for the last couple of weeks made her realise that she had done her best and she would again. There would need to be adjustments but she could do it. If Marina continued to help out at the boarding house, she would be fine. If not, she would still be fine.

Mary packed her bags slowly. It had been three days since her father's funeral and Mary felt her mother was ready for her to leave too. She had helped her pack her father's room away, leaving the equipment spotless when the hospital people came to retrieve them. She didn't know if she could get a train that late in the afternoon, but she wanted to have it booked for at least the next day. Her skin twitched with excitement at the thought of seeing Lawrence again but her heart was heavy. She didn't know what this would mean for them. She wondered how she was going to bring it up with Lawrence, not to mention her daughters. *Oh, hello, everyone. I've missed you all. By the way, there's going to be a baby!* It sounded absurd. How would Marina react? Maybe she would go back to being peculiar again and just when she had finally come out of her shell. She sighed and sat down on the bed. She would have to deal with whatever came. She had been away for nearly three weeks and she missed home madly. But she knew she was also dreading it now.

First, she had to tell her mother that she was leaving. She didn't think that would be a problem. Julia didn't seem terribly interested in what she did anyway. She and her mother had barely exchanged a handful of words since she'd been there, and Mary knew things had not changed since she had left them so long ago. Curt good mornings and silent dinners were their interchanges in the last few weeks. She walked into the kitchen where her mother sat at the table with a cigarette in her hand, absently flicking the pages of a magazine.

'Mother, I'm going to go down to the station to book my ticket.'

'Can you stay a little longer?' Her mother didn't look up from her magazine.

Mary was taken aback. She thought her mother would be dying to get rid of her. 'Do you need me to do anything else?' Mary thought she had done everything her mother had wanted her there for.

'I am moving to Lake Shore Home. They have accepted me.'

'Lake Shore?'

'The nursing home.'

'Why?'

Her mother looked down at her walking stick. 'Well, you may as well know. I'm going to be following him soon, your father, to wherever he has gone.'

'What?' Mary collapsed into the chair opposite her mother and stared at her, her mouth open.

Her mother tapped at her chest, a smile that resembled relief on her face. 'My ticker. Heart disease or some new-fangled something.'

'It's not new-fangled anything!'

'Yes, these days, they come up with all sorts of things to get rid of you.'

Mary wanted to argue. She wanted to tell her mother that she had done it to herself. She was sick because of what she had put her body through, through her drinking and smoking and doing whatever else to have fun with her father. It was no coincidence they were both going at the same time. But she knew it was more the resentment she felt towards them that made her want to say that. 'What did the doctors say?'

'What I told you.'

Mary moved into carer mode. Things needed to be done and her mother was certainly not after her sympathy. 'Okay, so what do you need me to do?'

'Maybe help me to get rid of everything here, sell the house maybe. I'm supposed to move out of here in two months.'

'I have to get home. I have a place to run. I have to check up on the girls ...'

'Go then if you want, I can do it myself,' said her mother. 'Never needed you before. Don't need you now.' She thumped the walking stick on the floor. She leaned up on it and walked out of the room.

Mary sat there in silence. At first she wondered how to say no to her mother. Perhaps she could come to stay with them at Righteous Creek. She could probably try to talk her into that even though the thought of her mother living with her was jarring. But a little sense of relief began to seep through her. She didn't want to stay here for a minute more, but maybe this was what she needed. Some time to get her head around everything, some space from Lawrence. A plan about how to deal with this new development. She put her hand to her stomach and felt guilt at her thoughts. This was a baby that was already loved but the situation needed contemplation. But when she thought about it she really was being a coward. She just wanted to put off the inevitable.

She walked down to the phone booth that afternoon and called home. She hoped Lawrence was at the house. She needed to hear his voice, to feel some comfort. He may not be here with her, but she longed to hear him, to know he missed her and needed her. Being in that cold, lonely house was depressing. Marina answered the phone, a subdued Marina, unlike the way she'd been in the past couple of weeks. Mary asked her what was wrong, but there was a short silence and Lawrence came on the phone.

'What's the matter?' Mary was worried. 'Is she okay?'

'A spat with a boy,' said Lawrence. 'She's fine.'

'Lawrence, you must let me know what's going on.'

'Just girl stuff, I think. I can see how tough you have it.' He forced a little chuckle.

'Are you there a lot?'

'I'm trying to come up a little more, help Marina out, you know.'

'Thank you. You really don't have to do that. She seems to like being in charge.' Mary chuckled. 'How are you?'

'Missing you like the devil. When are you getting home?'

Mary's heart warmed at the way he said 'home', like it was *their* home, not just hers. She had determined to get things out in the open when she returned, but now … 'I … um, I miss you too,' she said despite herself. 'There's a lot going on here. Mother wants me to stay a little longer. Maybe a couple of months or so, I'd guess.'

There was a silence on the other end of the line.

'Lawrence?'

'I'm here,' he said.

'I need to stay a little longer,' she repeated.

'I heard you.' His voice was soft, disappointed. 'You do what you need to do. Everything is fine here.'

She got off the phone and cried into her hands.

CHAPTER 32

The next couple of weeks were spent clearing out the house, cleaning it from top to bottom, Mary's mother watching and trying to help. Their relationship had improved but only slightly and only because her mother's grief over losing her husband needed venting.

'He was the love of my life,' she said one evening while they ate dinner together. Mary nodded, not sure of how to respond. 'I wanted him from the moment I saw him, tall, dark, handsome, but he only had eyes for me.'

'I know how that feels,' replied Mary and was surprised that she hadn't thought about Gary, that Lawrence was the one who now entered her mind. She liked how that felt but a fear nevertheless coursed through her veins.

'Do you?' Her mother studied her and Mary felt her cheeks redden. This topic was never one she discussed with anyone, let alone her mother. She nodded.

'I understand how you feel, Mother. I really do.'

'The man you talk of. Is he the father of your baby?'

Mary looked at her in confusion. What was her mother talking about? 'Yes, Gary is the father of Lucille and Marina. What do you mean?'

220

'I mean the baby that's in you now.' Her mother smiled sardonically.

Mary dropped her head and her hand went to her belly. 'How did you know?'

Her mother shrugged. 'Does he know?'

'No.'

'Is that why you agreed to stay?'

Mary considered her answer. There was no point in lying. 'Partly, yes. But I wanted to stay to help you. I would have anyway.'

Her mother nodded and another silence ensued, but it was a comfortable one now. Mary was thankful her mother didn't ask any more questions. Mary didn't even know how far along she was, but suspected it had to have been at least a couple of months. Her stomach was still flat and it probably would be another few months before she began to show.

She called the boarding house less regularly now, her fear of breaking down and telling Lawrence keeping her clear of them. When she did call, the conversations were quick, all ending with 'When are you coming home?' And Mary wasn't sure of that answer at all now. She still hadn't made a plan and the sale of her mother's house was taking longer than expected. A few potential buyers came around, looked about the place and didn't make an offer. Mary and her mother continued to try to make the place as appealing as possible, trying to work out ways to entice a buyer, but the only thing that would was a drop in price and her mother was not having any of that. Mary didn't ask why but wondered about it.

The nursing home was being kept on hold for her and

they certainly wouldn't wait very long. Mary couldn't understand why her mother wouldn't just sell the place for whatever she got for it. It wasn't like she needed the money for anything; in fact, that was the only thing she found becoming about her parents, that they had no issues with stinginess. They may not have given her their love, but they did provide her with everything, and she barely heard them complain about money, even though she knew they didn't have much of it. In fact, a month after she was at her mother's house, she answered the door to two deliverymen, and a piano. Her heart jumped out of her chest and when she thanked her mother, the woman just shrugged.

'You always loved to play that old thing we had when you were a child.'

And Mary played. It took away the dullness of the days, brought memories of Gary, of Lawrence, of Mrs Davis, and often, she would find her mother standing behind her, a look of pride on her face. But when Mary looked up at her, her mother quickly hobbled out of the room. But she worried. Every evening, every night, she battled with herself. Her part in deceiving the father of her baby and worse, having to break the news to him.

It turned out she didn't have to.

At the beginning of her third month in Perth, Mary went down to the phone booth to make her call to the boarding house. She dreaded it now, but it was nice to talk to Marina and Lucille when she came down for her semester break. Sometimes the Davises came on the phone and begged her to come home as they missed her. She missed them all, especially Lucille, but she never mentioned anything to Lucille in the letters she mailed to her every couple of weeks and enjoyed the news that Lucille sent. She was learning a lot. It was tough but she was counting the days until she came home for the semester break. She wished she could come to Perth, but on her part-time salary, she couldn't afford to, especially by air.

And Sophie! She had been mad as a hatter when she had come to stay at Jesse's Boarding. 'Come back,' she had ordered. 'I'm stuck here with a bunch of crazy people and you're not here to help me!' She had softened when Mary explained why she needed to stay, carefully leaving out the part about the little thing in her tummy.

Mary smiled now. She missed her friend and hoped she was there. Sophie could always make her laugh. She dialled home.

'Hi, darling,' she said when Marina answered the phone.

'Mum, I'm having a baby,' announced Marina.

Mary almost dropped the receiver and quickly brought it back to her ear. 'What? Say that again.'

'I'm going to have a baby. I'm pregnant!' Marina's voice was smiling, and Mary leaned against the glass of the phone booth to steady herself.

'How?' What a dumb question! But she didn't know what to say.

'Mum! When are you coming home? I have news for you. So much news.'

'But who? What's going on there?'

'And I'm getting married too!'

'Marina!'

'It's Lawrence, Mum. We're going to have a child

223

together. And he asked me to marry him. We're not going to wait either. The baby is due in September, I think,' Marina rushed on.

Mary felt her stomach drop to the ground and leaned on the cool glass, her legs threatening to crumble beneath her. Her throat was tight and her face was breaking out in a sweat. No, something wasn't right.

'Mum, are you there?' Marina sounded concerned now. 'I know this is unexpected but it's the seventies. Premarital sex exists. And no one will know any better if we are married.' She paused. 'Mum ...'

'I'm here,' Mary whispered.

'Please be happy for me, Mum. Lawrence is a great guy. You know it too. And I know he's a little older than me, but I love him. I've always loved him.'

I loved him first, Mary wanted to yell into the phone, but she didn't. 'If you love him and he loves you, just be happy.'

'Will you come back? For the wedding? I know I said all that stuff about the seventies, but Lawrence doesn't want there to be a stain on my name or something like that. So it will have to be soon. We were thinking the first of March.'

'I don't know if I can get back by then,' said Mary. 'I have to go, but congratulations and I'll let you know what happens.'

'Okay, I love you, Mum,' said Marina and Mary squeezed the tears from her eyes.

'I love you too,' she replied and hung up the phone. She came out of the phone booth and sat on a bench at the bus stop trying to come to terms with the conversation she just had with her daughter. Marina … and Lawrence! How could this have happened? Could Marina have been so oblivious to what had been going on with her and Lawrence? Or did she just prefer not to see it?

The cold of the evening came and stung her, but Mary sat on that bench trying to piece together how this could have happened. Had she been that much of a fool? She thought about how Marina had been with Lawrence since the day he arrived. She'd attached herself to him almost immediately, and she only now remembered the resentful looks from Marina when Mary and Lawrence talked out on the porch or came back from a walk. She almost choked on a laugh that inadvertently erupted her mouth. And she thought it was Lucille who had designs on Lawrence. A teenage crush, she had put it down to, and for Lucille it was. But Marina? Had she been nursing these feelings for him all along? Had they grown with the frequency of his visits?

And what about Lawrence? Her heart hurt and a burst of anger rumbled through her body. How could he? How could he do that to Mary and take advantage of her daughter? After all that had happened between them? But something kept nudging at Mary. She knew Lawrence, or thought she knew him, and there was a reason he was doing this. But to get Marina pregnant? How could that have happened? Could she have seduced him? Well, if he could be seduced by someone else, and of all people, Mary's daughter, then she really never knew him at all.

Again a scoff emitted from her throat. Age. That's what it eventually came down to. She knew it would. It just happened sooner rather than later. And so soon! It wasn't a month ago when Lawrence was professing his love to her over the phone.

How could he? She couldn't understand how she had been so wrong about him. And now she was pregnant with his child. Why had she been so stupid to give herself to him when she knew better?

She took a deep breath and let it out, wrapping her scarf around her, as she rose from her seat. Should she go back for the wedding? That was a week away. And September! That was when her own baby was due.

She would have to go back, she decided. Attend the wedding and return back here. She couldn't let them see what was going on with her. She swiped away the tears and returned to her mother's house, a place she knew she would be staying for a quite a while.

CHAPTER 33

It was a beautiful day, the sun piercing the earth and the birds chirping with glee, when Mary alighted the train, physically tired and mentally exhausted. For a split second, Mary felt like she was in a movie, where everything was going to turn into a happy ever after, where the awful nightmare was just that. Then she returned to reality when she saw Lucille waving and running towards her. Her face broke out in a stupid grin and she rushed to her, throwing her arms around her daughter, hugging her so tight and for so long that Lucille laughed and pulled out of her embrace.

It had been a difficult trip. She still had morning sickness and most of the train ride was spent in the bathroom clutching her stomach and throwing up. And when the train chugged to a stop in Geelong, she knew she was in for a long, hard day. She was going to watch the man she was in love with marry her daughter. And she would smile and hug and return to Perth the next day.

She had been dreading the half-hour drive to Righteous Creek with Lucille, steeling herself for the countless questions that would be thrown her way. But she didn't have much to tell Lucille. She knew nothing, except that Marina had seduced Lawrence or vice versa. She didn't want to even think about it, how it happened, how wrong she had been, what an idiot she had been.

'What the hell is going on, Mum?' Lucille blurted when they had put Mary's overnight case in the boot and gotten into the car.

Mary tried to smile. Her back was in pain and she was about to be sick again. 'Your sister is getting married,' she said.

'Yes, I know. That's why we are here. But he's supposed to be getting married to you!'

'Oh, Lucille,' Mary said, trying to laugh lightly. 'What would give you such a silly idea?'

'Really, Mum?' Lucille looked at her mother and frowned. 'This is all a bit sudden, isn't it? You're gone for three months, and she's pregnant and getting married to Lawrence.'

'It was a bit sudden,' Mary admitted. 'But things happen. People fall in love all the time.'

'Oh, don't be so calm. You have to be seething. And of all people, Lawrence!'

'We can't help who we love,' said Mary, not wanting to continue this line of conversation. 'How's the nursing going?'

'Nearly done,' said Lucille. 'And I've also got news.' She smiled. 'Raymond has asked me to marry him.'

'Raymond?'

'Don't you remember I told you about him?'

'Yes, of course. Oh Lucille, I'm so happy for you. Will he be at the wedding?'

'No, he couldn't make it.'

They drove home, Lucille telling Mary all about her course, her apartment and about Raymond, and Mary hoped her daughter would keep the happiness that seemed so fleeting in her own life.

'I am returning to Perth tomorrow,' said Mary.

'What? Why?'

'Because my mother is dying. She has no one.'

'That's her own fault.'

'Lu, don't be so ungiving.'

'What did they ever give you?'

'My life. And because of that, you girls.'

By the time they rolled up to the house, Mary had asked Lucille to stop three times so she could have a break, once even throwing up. When she got back in the car, Lucille eyed her suspiciously. 'What's up with you?'

'It was a long trip and you know how I can get travel sick.'

'I've never seen you travel sick. In fact, I don't think I've ever seen you throw up.' Her eyes widened. 'Mum, are you …?'

Mary tried to laugh. 'Stop it!'

'You forget I am nearly a fully qualified nurse.'

'You forget that I'm your mother,' said Mary sternly.

'What are you going to do?'

'Attend my daughter's wedding,' she replied, letting Lucille know that the subject was closed. She hated to lie to Lucille, but right now she had to protect herself and Marina. 'Funny,' she said, trying to lighten the mood with a change of subject. 'When Lawrence first came into our lives, I thought it would be you who would fall in love with him.'

'I did flirt with him,' replied Lucille, acknowledging that her mother was not going to budge. 'Oh, wasn't I so silly?'

Mary turned to her daughter. 'Lucille, in case I don't tell you often enough, I'm so proud of you.'

The car rolled into the driveway and Mary felt a sense of happiness, of home, but now it was a feeling mixed with confusion, anger and humiliation. She was relieved Lawrence's car wasn't in the car park. As she was getting out of the car, Sophie was already upon them and threw her arms around Mary.

'Where have you been?' she scolded and punched Mary playfully on her arm.

'Why are you here?' Mary was ecstatic to see her friend and her sense of being alone was slowly dissipating.

'I've been here for the last week. And there's a wedding,' she said, taking Mary's arm in hers, while Lucille unloaded Mary's suitcase. 'What the hell happened? I've been gone for a couple of months and everything's changed!'

'Long story,' said Mary, already weary. She would have to tell Sophie something but she was so tired, her mind and her body. And it was going to be a busy day. Maybe she would be gone before Sophie woke up tomorrow and she wouldn't have to explain anything at all. She walked into the back of the house to the hugs of the Davises and Moira, all of whom seemed to have missed her, and she went to her room, all of them following her, regaling stories of when she was away. She suddenly stopped at her bedroom door, wondering if it was still hers. Maybe Lawrence and Marina had taken it over. Lucille smiled at her and took her suitcase in and when she walked in, everything was as normal, unchanged since she had left. She hadn't seen Lawrence or Marina yet and wondered where they were. She was dreading seeing either of them and wanted to keep away until it all began but she knew she couldn't hole up in her room. Everyone would be suspicious and she needed everything to seem normal.

'Where is everyone?' she asked Lucille, who sat on her bed while Mary unpacked.

'They are out the front. It's only two hours before the celebrant gets here.'

'Oh,' said Mary, feeling sad that she didn't get to help organise her daughter's wedding. She sighed. Of course it was probably better she didn't.

Mary went to the front porch where she could see Marina setting up fairy lights around a white marquee with two girls Mary had never seen before. She leaned on the frame of the door, resting her aching head. She felt Sophie nudge her. 'What's going on, Mary?'

'It's my daughter's wedding,' said Mary, taking a deep breath, and stepped out into the beach, the place she loved so much.

****

'A beautiful wedding,' said Mary, as Lucille drove her back to the station early the next morning.

Lucille pouted. 'You know when you said you had two beautiful children? Well, you should have stopped at one.'

'Oh, stop it.'

'Mum, seriously. I don't think it's Lawrence's child.'

'What?'

'A few months ago, Marina told me about a guy she was seeing, a serious boyfriend. She thought she was pregnant at the end of last year too.'

'How do I not know about this?'

'Because she didn't want to upset you. But it was a false alarm, so it didn't matter anyway.'

'But Lawrence?' Mary couldn't understand what was happening.

'I think he's being gallant.' She rolled her eyes. 'Mum, we should do something.'

'Your sister is happily married now,' said Mary. 'And so is Lawrence.'

'Yeah, to the wrong woman.'

'Oh, Lucille.'

'I saw how he looked at you, Mum. He is not in love with her.'

'You're seeing things,' replied Mary. 'I don't think we should talk like this anymore. Marriage is for life, and he is now your sister's life.'

'But …'

'No, Lucille. Subject closed. Forever.'

But when the train rolled out of the station, Mary put her head in her hands and cried. Like she never had before. Not even when Gary died. She thought of Lawrence, how he had walked down the aisle just before Marina had and stopped for a moment beside her chair. She didn't dare look up at him and he continued past. And Marina, floating down the aisle, looking so radiant, so beautiful, her slim body encased in a sheath of cream silk, a crown of flowers in her hair, her feet bare as she walked, no, pranced down the aisle, smiling to the few guests on either side of her. And even though her heart was breaking, it also soared at the thought that Lawrence had brought life back to her daughter. Mary held back her tears, even when Lucille squeezed her hand on one side of her, and Sophie did on the other. And she watched as the sun began to set behind them, knowing it was the end of all her hopes. The ceremony was over in a matter of minutes and then the chairs were pulled apart to form a circle. Someone brought out the radio and the music began, the few guests already ready to party their way through the night.

Mary was brought back to the first time she danced with Lawrence, in the moonlight, on a night much like this one. But then she had been excited, every fibre of her being exhilarated by the man who ignited the spark in her. Today she should have felt joy for her daughter; and she did, but with the pain of watching the man she loved marry another woman, her heart was torn into a billion strips.

She watched as they had their first dance, Marina, her face leaned against her husband's chest and Lawrence, looking over her head as he gazed at Mary with such despair. She held his eyes for a moment and her body wanted to give way. She got up and headed to the beach, away from this, whatever this was. She walked along the shore and stopped to try to gain the calm she always felt when she stood here. Then she kept walking, in the dark, to the rock, even though she knew it was the last place she should go, but she stopped again. That wouldn't be right. She had to forget he existed as her lover. He was now her son-in-law, the father of her daughter's child. And her own child too, she thought, bitterly.

She stood at the water's edge and rested her hand on her belly. She was in a predicament. She would have to make up a story, have the baby in Perth, come back and by then she would work something out, something to tell everyone. She didn't hear him through the sound of the water that lapped at her feet. She felt his hand on her arm and knew it was him before she turned to see him standing there, beautiful in his loose blue shirt, opened at the collar, his hair loosely hanging beneath his ears. She had the impulse to grab a lock of it, take him in her arms, tell him to forget everything, to run away with her.

She didn't. She shook him off and looked away from him, back towards the sea. It was not calm now.

'Mary,' he began.

'Congratulations,' she said quickly before he could offer any sorry excuse of an explanation. 'I am so very happy for you … and Marina.'

'Please, you need to listen to me, Mary.'

'No, I don't actually,' she said and started back to the house. She felt his hand on her elbow and she shook it off again.

'Just for a minute. I need to explain …'

She turned to face him. 'No, Lawrence, you don't.' She strode back to the house, relieved when she saw the merry lights ahead, knowing he wouldn't try to talk to her in the presence of others.

Now, she thought about what Lucille had said. Did he marry Marina because she was pregnant—with someone else's child? And what about the father? Well, whatever it was, he had made a decision and his need to save Marina was greater than his need for her. He had made his choice, knowing well that he would never have her again.

CHAPTER 34

It would be more than a year before Mary returned to Righteous Creek. Her mother had passed away some weeks earlier and Mary had sold the house, promptly writing a cheque for the amount to the respite home who had sent nurses to help her care for her mother. Her mother admitted she had wanted to die in the house she shared with her husband and Mary felt a sense of closure allowing her that. She spent the last year getting to know her mother, forgiving her for not loving her as much as she should have and when she had her child, a beautiful boy she called Brayden, Gary's middle name, her mother became the grandmother she should have been, even in her sorry state. Mary had made a few friends at the local club where she took her mother every couple of weeks, and after she had the baby, she and her mother had bonded even further, Julia never looking more alive than she had, even in her youth. Mary had never seen her so excited about anything apart from her husband, and she allowed her mother to spoil the baby, cradling him when he cried, cooing to him as she walked shakily with him on her good hip. They spent time together, sewing and knitting clothes and booties for Brayden, and when her mother passed, Mary felt something she never thought she would feel from her mother. It was something akin to love.

She had called home every month and Marina gave her the news about her burgeoning pregnancy, Mary listening with her teeth tightly against her lips, her heart in agony, mixed with a joy for her daughter who had found a reason to be happy. When Lawrence picked up the phone, she hung up and tried again the next week. She was not ready to have any sort of conversation with him. And when she received a letter from him at her mother's house, she was tempted to read it, to hear what he had to say, to read the words that came from his hand, but she knew she shouldn't. He was now the husband of her daughter, and to entertain any thoughts of him other than that was wrong. She tore it up, still in its envelope, into little bits and flushed it down the toilet.

The boarding house was doing as well as it was before she had left and Mary suspected it had more to do with Lawrence than Marina. And when Marina had her child, a boy she called Darren, Mary was tempted to go back, to see her first grandchild, to be the mother and grandmother she always wanted to be. Close, loving, giving. But the time was not right yet.

'It's the name of that guy!' yelled Lucille when Mary called her at her apartment in Melbourne. 'Darren. The same guy she was with the earlier time. She's nuts, Mum!'

'Lu, that's enough.' Every time Mary spoke to Lucille, her daughter harped on about the farce that was her sister's marriage and even though in the back of Mary's mind she knew, there was not much that could be done about anything.

'But Mum …'

'How are you doing?'

'Looking forward to the wedding, my wedding,' she said and Mary could hear the smile in her voice. 'I was hoping to have it at home. I don't know when though. We haven't set a date, but I want to finish my studies first.'

'I'm so happy, Lu,' cried Mary, her heart soaring for her daughter.

'I've got to go, but when do you think you will go home?'

Mary hesitated. 'I have to. Soon, I guess.'

'Are you worried about seeing them?' Lucille's voice was soft, worried.

Mary hesitated. 'Maybe ...'

'Take back what's yours, Mum.'

Mary didn't know what she meant. Her life at the boarding house, or Lawrence. The latter was certainly not an option. But she couldn't just return with a child without an explanation about his existence. An adopted son, a motherless child whom she couldn't leave in a foster home. She would take it to the grave with her and not buckle for anyone. For a while, Mary even considered staying in Perth, away from everything she adored. But she knew she had to go back. As much as she resented the situation, it was one that had to be faced. She'd never shied away from her circumstances before, and there'd been worse. When it was time to return, she was ready.

CHAPTER 35

Her train arrived in Melbourne early in the morning and there would be a two-hour gap before the next one to Geelong where Marina was supposed to collect her for the drive to Righteous Creek. Lucille had arranged to visit Mary at the station in Melbourne, and to take her to breakfast. She was unable to drive her to Righteous Creek as she was about to start a shift, but she wanted to see her mother. It had been so long, over a year, since the fateful wedding and Mary couldn't wait to see Lucille again.

Mary cradled Brayden, just under six months old, a calm little fellow, who had barely cried on the long journey. He cooed at her now and helped calm the butterflies that were battling in her stomach. It was the first explanation she would have to give, and she was glad it was to Lucille. She sat on the wooden seat, eagerly awaiting her daughter, looking on either side of her, a lump lodged in her throat. And then she saw Lucille hurrying towards her, her mouth open wide in a smile, which turned to an O when she saw what Mary held in her arms. She slowed and put her hand to her mouth, her eyes opening wide. She stopped in her tracks for a short moment and then in a few large strides she reached her mother. Mary's heart melted as she felt her daughter's arms encircle her and she clutched at her sleeve, not wanting to let go. She knew she missed her, she just never realised how much.

Lucille stepped back and looked down at Brayden, who was gurgling. She took him from her mother's arms and placed him on her shoulder and kissed his ear. 'For a moment I thought this was Darren,' she said almost to herself. 'This is not Darren.' She brought the baby back down and cradled him, gazing at him.

'No, he's not,' said Mary. 'Surprise.' She tried to smile.

'Who is he?' asked Lucille, patting the chubby cheek. 'How old is he?'

'Brayden. His name is Brayden. He's six months old. A baby who was to be abandoned. I couldn't let him be …'

Lucille was staring at her mother with narrowed eyes. 'Mother! Why do you lie to me?' she cried. 'This is your baby. He has your eyes, and my mouth!' She looked at Brayden again. 'And Lawrence's jaw.'

'What are you talking about?' Mary laughed nervously, somehow knowing Lucille was never going to be fooled. She was too shrewd.

'You were pregnant when you came down for the wedding, weren't you?'

'No, of course not. Don't be silly, Lucille.'

'Mum, please stop lying to me. You can lie to Marina and Lawrence and whoever else you want to, but you can confide in me. I won't let you down, not like she did.'

Mary slumped her shoulders and set herself down on the wooden bench. Tears flowed down her cheeks and she shook with utter relief, the burden a little lighter. Lucille sat beside her and took her in her arms. 'You can't tell anyone,' whispered

Mary. 'This cannot affect Marina and Lawrence.'

'Oh Mum, why are you always protecting her?' Lucille looked down at Brayden.

'Because she's my child and I vowed to protect you both.'

'But she has been selfish, not thinking of anyone but herself.' Lucille paused. 'Do you know she knew about you and Lawrence?'

Mary raised her head in surprise. 'What?'

'I think everyone knew. You thought you were being careful but you couldn't hide it as well as you thought you did. Sneaking away, staring at each other, trying not to talk in front of people ...' Mary put her head in her hands and shook it and Lucille rubbed her back.

'Why do you think she knew though?'

'She used to watch you walk away together and she always had that look on her face, like, you know, like she was mad.'

'She has some problems. She had been so down that she was doing things that were dangerous. If this is what it took to complete her, then it's a small price to pay to protect my family.'

Lucille sighed with resignation. 'Don't go back there,' she said suddenly. 'Stay here in Melbourne with me. Ray will be so happy to meet you, to have you staying with us when we get married. And if you don't want to live with us, you can get your own place ...'

'The boarding house is all I have,' said Mary.

'No!' cried Lucille. 'You have so much more. You can get a job here, you can study if you want. There are so many things ...'

'I have to go back. It's still my home.'

'But living with them?'

'I'm over him, Lu. I will be fine.' As she said it, Mary was not sure she was, so she put the idea in the back of her mind.

'You know they sleep in separate rooms, don't you?' Mary didn't want to know anything of the sort. 'She complained about it. That he wouldn't give himself to her.'

Mary didn't want to think about that. It was none of her business. 'That's enough, Lu,' she said with finality.

****

She steeled herself when she got to the station in Geelong, in anticipation of seeing Marina. She felt a sorrow that her child had taken her happiness from her, and knowingly, from what Lucille had said. But when she got off the train, the baby in his carriage, she saw Lawrence standing at the platform, his eyes wide in astonishment, his jaw slack.

Her heart sank. She knew she wasn't over him but she took a deep breath and strode over quickly. As they walked to the car, he kept his eyes on the pram, and Mary dared not look in his direction.

He settled the baby on Mary's lap, wordless, and they drove home in silence. Home. His, hers ... and Marina's. When they reached the house, he turned off the ignition and put his hand on hers. 'We will be out of here within the week.'

Mary nodded. She didn't protest. She knew it was best if he weren't around, especially now after feeling tingles on the back of her spine for the last half hour's drive. He was so close to her and it had taken everything not to reach out and touch his face, the stubble on his face making him more attractive than she remembered. The scent of him so near, was overwhelming and she had bury her nose in Brayden's hair just so she didn't feel the need to get closer to him.

Mary entered the house to a barrage of hugs and exclamations and she knew she had done the right thing. She was home. After explaining her story to the Davises and Sophie, who was now a permanent resident, having taken over most of the house's chores, Mary sat on the porch, rocking her child in her arms, and stared out at the familiar sight of the beach, the water so blue, so calm, her place. But it was Marina's home too. How could she let her move away from everything that kept her sane? But Lawrence was right. He knew they couldn't live in the same house as her, but it was unfair that they be the ones to move out. It had to be her. Marina was thriving; running Jesse's Boarding had been good for her. Her baby had been good for her. She was whole and Mary didn't want to ruin any of the things that made her happy.

She thought about Gary again, wishing someone else could have seen his plight, known that he needed more help. She should have known; he may still have been here with her if she had done something. But she had this time, with Marina.

Marina came out and sat beside Mary, who took her hand. Marina let her hand be held by her mother and Mary's heart warmed.

'Where's Darren?' asked Mary. The little boys had been enamoured with each other when they first met and she hoped they would be great little playmates.

'Lawrence has him,' said Marina, finally retrieving her hand.

'He's beautiful, Marina. I wish I could have been here when you had him.'

'No, I guess you were too busy having a baby of your own.'

Mary flinched. 'I didn't,' she said.

'Right.' Marina fingered the cushion she had placed on her lap. Mary knew her daughter wanted to say more but she was also afraid of what may come out of her.

'Want to help me cook?' Mary asked, standing up.

'I'm going out for a bit. I think Mrs Davis wanted to make something special for your return,' she said, with emphasis on 'return'. Marina was evidently the only one not happy about Mary's return.

'Where are you going?'

'Just out,' Marina replied evasively.

'Okay,' Mary said. Her daughter was an adult and it was clear she didn't appreciate her mother questioning her.

'Lawrence says we are moving out,' Marina said when Mary got to the door.

'You don't have to do that,' said Mary. 'I'm going to stay with Lucille in Melbourne for a while. I think I need a change of pace and Lu asked me to stay.'

She saw Marina's head bob up and down and knew it was the right decision. She would leave as soon as she found a place in Melbourne. She had to get herself organised and was glad she had a telephone to make those plans. Lucille was excited for her to come.

'I'm setting up the lounge room for you. It's a small place, but …'

'Lu, I need a place of my own. If you can help me to find one, that would be the best thing.'

'But why?'

'Because it's not just me. It's the baby too.'

'Okay, Mum; when will you be coming?'

'As soon as possible.'

'I will let you know when I get one. Mum,' said Lucille, 'you're doing the right thing.'

Mary nodded and knew she was.

CHAPTER 36

It was the very next day when Lucille called.

'Got it,' she said, her voice high with excitement. 'You can come the day after tomorrow.'

'Wow, that was quick,' said Mary, wondering if it was too soon, but she knew the sooner it was the better. She had a tough time trying to stay out of the way of Lawrence and Marina. Sophie had been livid when she told her of her plans.

'I can't stay here, Sophie,' she had said.

'I've missed you, my friend, don't go.'

'I have to.' She held her friend's hand. 'But I will be in Melbourne and we can go out and get our hair and nails done, and go shopping together.'

'Does that mean we can't sit on the beach and talk like we used to? I have been waiting for you to come back to do that.'

'We can tonight,' said Mary. And they did; they talked of old times, of Sophie's decision to move to the theatre, rather than seek film roles that took her away from here. 'This has become your home too,' said Mary.

'Yes, but it won't be without you. But I will stay because

I know you will be back. This will always be your home.'

Mary wasn't so sure anymore, but she nodded. She would miss this place terribly, everything about it, even the bad memories it brought. Maybe that was her lot. She only had one chance at real love and that was Gary. To ask for it to happen again would be gluttonous.

The night before she left, Mary felt a strong desire to walk along the beach. She had to take one last look at her place, the place she loved so much, that wasn't hers anymore. She watched the waves lap the sand and convinced herself that the city Melbourne was not so far from the beach too. She could still sit and watch the world and the waves go by. She found herself at the rock and sat upon it, thinking about the last time she was here, when life seemed so full of hope. When love still had meaning and …

'Mary.' She turned to find Lawrence behind her and she stiffened. She hoped he would continue to avoid her, but something deep in her suspected she had come here because he would find her here. 'You have a child.'

'I adopted a child,' she replied.

'I know he's my son,' he said.

She thought it pointless to lie to him and remained silent.

'I love you, Mary.' She felt hot tears roll down her face.

'I love you, Lawrence,' she replied. 'The first and last time I will say those words. Please don't ever say it to me again either.'

His hands were on her shoulders and she let them remain there, knowing how terribly wrong it was to allow him to touch her. But she knew by now why he had done what he'd done. He didn't have to explain it to her and he seemed to know it too. They were both protecting her child. He didn't try to offer any explanation. She turned to him and let him rest his lips on hers. Then she got off the rock and walked out of his life.

EPILOGUE

She sat on their rock, letting the breeze move through her hair, and she closed her eyes, inhaling the scent of the sea. She was home, had been for nearly a month before she had the bravery to return here to this place that was theirs, their rock. And rightly so. It brought him back to her again, memories of their time here so vivid, it seemed like yesterday when he first found her here.

In the past three years, she had been not happy, but content. Living in Melbourne, away from her demons had been just what she'd needed. She didn't have the constant reminders of her dead husband and the man who had abandoned her. No, she knew that was harsh. He did it for her. She realised that now, knew it then, but knew there was also nothing to be done about it. But Lawrence had given her the ability to move on from Gary, to remember him with love, as she always would.

She even dated a few times in Melbourne, a nice man at the place she worked, a boarding house of all things. She chuckled at that, knowing it was what she wanted to do forever, take care of people, talk to them, be a refuge for the people who needed a home, those with and those without the means to pay for it. It didn't work out with Robbie either, or Marty, the man who owned the house. But she also knew her heart was now open to whatever came.

But the only thing that came to her thoughts and into her heart was Lawrence and when she heard from Lucille that Marina had taken off to God knows where, leaving the baby with Lawrence, some two years ago, she wanted to run back to him, to cry with him, to help him through it. The man had enough heartache, but at least this time, he had his son; no, not his son, Marina's son, Mary's grandchild. But she didn't go to him, hoping that Marina would grow up at some time and realise what she'd done, but she also knew the girl was beyond self-centred. It wasn't about her mental health; she was nothing like Gary. She was selfish and Mary blamed herself for allowing her daughter to be that way. But it was the way it was and she just hoped her daughter would finally find satisfaction in something. Not even taking Lawrence from Mary had fulfilled her.

She still stayed in Melbourne, after that, knowing Lawrence had returned to his home. She needed to have this time to herself. At times, she felt guilty for keeping Lawrence's son from him, but he had known Brayden was his son. And he had known that to fight for him would be to cause more hurt to everyone around them. Mary appreciated that and loved him all the more for it.

Love. It was all around her. She was with her family, the Davises, Sophia, Moira and soon, Lucille would be coming to live in Righteous Creek with her own baby girl, having secured a position at the local hospital, while she studied to obtain her specialty as a mental health nurse. There was music at the house, laughter, dancing, playing with Brayden, Mrs Davis excited she had a new student for piano lessons.

When she went to town, she ignored the looks of people she had known all her life, when they glanced at her in judgement as she pushed her child in his stroller. She didn't owe them any explanation and never gave it a second thought. She knew they had lost their power over her and she could really now say she didn't give a damn about those petty people. She even bumped into Virginia in town and nodded and smiled at her warmly. Virginia looked away quickly, her eyes fearful, but Mary didn't want to scare her or hurt her. She had done that all to herself and Mary felt nothing but pity for the woman.

Mary was happy; she had everything she needed. She couldn't want for more than that. It was enough. Hopefully one day, she could have more to do with her grandchild, and in Lawrence's hands, she was sure he would turn out to be a wonderful man.

Lawrence. He changed her, she knew that. And she wished her heart didn't still thud at the thought of him. Maybe one day that would stop too. She pushed the thought aside and hopped off the rock.

The evening was cooling and it was time to head back to the house. She had forgotten to bring her shawl with her and rubbed at her arms, trying to settle the goosebumps that had taken hold. The sand was still warm though and she picked up her sandals, preferring to feel the comfort of the sand beneath her feet. She squished her feet in it and smiled and when she turned to head home, she froze, her belly feeling like it had fallen to the ground.

He was approaching, but she could see the question in his eyes, the hesitation in his stride. She found it hard to breathe and it took an effort to move her legs. But she did, towards him, slowly, carefully until she stood before him.

'Hello, Mary,' he said and everything that once existed was still there, imprinted on his face. The breeze blew a strand of hair across her face and he put out his hand to move it away from her eyes.

And she let him.

The End

ABOUT THE AUTHOR

Rita H Rowe is the author of contemporary works of fiction, which include *Never The Moon* and *Dancing With Ghosts*, her novels always spouting a touch of romance, between sometimes gritty themes.

She lives in Melbourne with her husband John and their two pampered dogs, Scarlett and Benji.

When she is not writing her heart out, Rowe can be found at her other job, teaching a wild and wonderful pack of secondary students at the local high school.

You can get in touch with Rowe on any of the following media sites:

Website: https://www.ritahrowe.com/

Facebook: https://www.facebook.com/ritahrowe/

Instagram: https://www.instagram.com/ritahrowe_writes/

OTHER NOVELS BY RITA H ROWE

Never The Moon

Two men who could not be more different.

One woman caught between them.

When Jennifer loses David, the love of her life, her world falls apart. Fleeing to New York for a fresh start, she meets Jack, rugged and handsome, everything she could hope for.

But her world is unexpectedly plunged into chaos and violence.

An abusive husband, a loveless marriage - and no way out.

When David comes back into her life; Jennifer is torn between the man she has always loved and a life she has now chosen...

Never The Moon interweaves the lives of Jennifer, David and Jack, revealing the power of love - and the destruction it can leave in its wake...

"Inspired and emotive, a great romance and heart-string tugger of a story...well done to a new voice of romance..." Debra, Indiebook reviewer.

She Remembered

Her beauty is a curse. Her memories a void.

Elena cannot remember. All she has are fragments of a past life that feel foreign to her, only glimpsed in fleeting moments through violent nightmares.

Struggling to put her life together and find acceptance, she takes comfort in Luke, a charming boy who seems to like her as much as she likes him. But nothing has ever come easily to Elena—and when she wakes up between blood-soaked sheets next to the body of a man recently stabbed, what little stability she had comes crashing down around her.

With no one to help her and nowhere to go, Elena has to salvage the broken pieces of her life all on her own. If only she could remember …

"I didn't predict the outcome and I thoroughly enjoyed the journey to get there. Definitely 5 stars from me." Umm Ibrahim – Amazon.

Dancing With Ghosts

Alex will never dance again.

Her parents and her dreams, all lost in one fateful night.

Unable to put her faith in love and happiness, not even

for Nicholas, the man she loves, she escapes to Chernut,

a country town far from the reminders of her past.

Here at the beautiful Lovelet Manor, inhabited by a

family who are as lost as she is, Alex finds solace

in the picturesque gardens of which she is caretaker,

accepting that her life can never be full again.

But when she meets Edward in the grand gazebo, she

discovers that her heart may not be done with her yet.

And for the first time in a long time,

she allows herself to be loved.

But is she losing her mind?

Will the ghosts of her past keep her running forever?

Or will Alex find herself before she runs out of time?

"Binge worthy. This is a ghost story with romance and characters so very real they are believable. I loved it." Amazon reviewer.

The Bad Seed

Love, betrayal and murder.

He's the new kid in town, complete with a sordid past and a tarnished family name, doomed to fail even before he begins. Jenna is the only person who sees beyond Joey's past and they fall deeply in love.

But there are already forces determined to separate the pair by any means necessary. Tommy, the thug, who is hell-bent on breaking Joey by brute force, Jenna's mother, whose connection with Joey cannot be ignored, and Joey's own past, the strongest weapon against them.

Only Tim, the local police officer, shows any compassion to the plight of Joey and Jenna, but is Tim all he seems? And what role will he play in their fate?

Can young love survive in a town filled with discrimination? Can Joey and Jenna get out before they fall apart, or is it already too late?

"A thrilling, heartbreaking read. I finished this book four days ago and I still can't get it out of my mind." Tina MK, Amazon.

Becoming Ruthless

When all the men she knows are liars, maybe it's time to become one too.

Ruth is young, excited about life and not looking for love. Yet love finds her, and Ruth is thrilled. But she is left devastated when she finds out that her the man she loves has deceived her. Still hopeful, she embarks on another relationship only to find herself in the same predicament.

Ruth becomes disenchanted with love and decides that if she can't beat them, she may as well join them and begins a journey that will change her very being and endanger her life.

Can Ruth find herself before it's too late? Or will she become what she has always despised—a loathsome liar?

"When I tell you I was excited for this book, I'm not kidding! I read it in one sitting, and absolutely could not put it down." Rebecca, Amazon.